Contents

Enid Blyton

THE SECRET STORIES

The Secret Island

Hodder
Children's
Books

HODDER CHILDREN'S BOOKS

First published in Great Britain in 1938 by Basil Blackwell
This edition published in 2016 by Hodder and Stoughton

7 9 10 8

Enid Blyton®
Enid Blyton's signature is a Registered Trademark of Hodder and Stoughton Limited
Text copyright Hodder and Stoughton
Illustrations copyright Hodder and Stoughton

A CIP catalogue record for this book
is available from the British Library.

ISBN 978 1 444 92110 6

Typeset in CaslonTwelve by Avon DataSet Ltd, Bidford on Avon, Warwickshire
Printed and bound in Great Britain by Clays Ltd, St Ives plc

The paper and board used in this book are from well-managed forests
and other responsible sources.

Hodder Children's Books
An imprint of
Hachette Children's Group
Part of Hodder & Stoughton
Carmelite House
50 Victoria Embankment
London EC4Y 0DZ

An Hachette UK Company
www.hachette.co.uk

www.hachettechildrens.co.uk

CHAPTER ONE

The Beginning of the Adventures

MIKE, PEGGY and Nora were sitting in the fields, talking together. They were very unhappy. Nora was crying, and would not stop. As they sat there, they heard a low call.

'Coo-ee!'

'There's Jack,' said Mike. 'Dry your eyes, Nora. Jack will cheer you up!'

A boy came running by the hedge and sat down by them. He had a face as brown as a berry and bright blue eyes that shone with mischief.

'Hello!' he said. 'What's up, Nora? Crying again?'

'Yes,' said Nora, wiping her eyes. 'Aunt Harriet yelled at me six times this morning because I didn't wash the curtains well enough. Look!' She showed him her hands which were red and sore from all the washing.

'It's a shame!' said Jack.

'If only our father and mother were here they wouldn't let us live like this,' said Mike. 'But somehow I don't believe they'll ever come back now.'

'How long is it since they've been gone?' asked Jack.

'It's over two years now,' said Mike. 'Dad built a fine new aeroplane, you know, and he set off to fly to Australia. Mother went with him, because she loves flying, too. They got nearly there – and then nothing more was heard of them!'

'And I know Aunt Harriet and Uncle Henry think they will never come back again,' said Nora, beginning to cry once more, 'or they would never treat us as they do.'

'Don't cry any more, Nora,' said Peggy. 'Your eyes will get so red and horrid. I'll do the washing instead of you next time.'

Jack put his arm round Nora. He liked her best of them all. She was the smallest, although she was Mike's twin. She had a little face, and a head of black curls. Mike was exactly like her, but bigger. Peggy had blonde hair and was a year older. Nobody knew how old Jack was. He didn't know himself. He lived with his grandfather on a tumble down farm, and worked as hard as a man, although he wasn't much bigger than Mike.

He had made friends with the children as they wandered through the fields. He knew how to catch rabbits. He knew how to catch fish in the river. He knew where the best nuts and blackberries were to be found. In fact, he knew everything, the children thought, even the names of all the birds that flew about the hedges, and the difference between a grass snake and an adder, and things like that.

Jack was always dressed in raggedy things, but the children didn't mind. His feet were bare, and his legs were scratched with brambles. He never grumbled; he never whined. He made a joke of everything, and he had been a good friend to the three miserable children.

'Ever since Aunt Harriet made up her mind that Mummy and Daddy wouldn't come back, she has been perfectly horrid,' said Nora.

'And so has Uncle Henry,' said Mike. 'We none of us go to school now, and I have to help Uncle in the fields from morning to night. I don't mind that, but I do wish Aunt Harriet wouldn't treat the two girls so badly. They are not very old, and she makes them do all the work of the house for her.'

'I do every bit of the washing now,' said Nora. 'I wouldn't mind the little things, but the sheets are so big and heavy.'

'And I do all the cooking,' said Peggy. 'Yesterday I burnt a cake because the oven got too hot, and Aunt Harriet sent me to bed for the rest of the day without anything to eat at all.'

'I climbed through the window and gave her some bread and cheese,' said Mike. 'And Uncle caught me and shook me so hard that I couldn't stand up afterwards.

I had to go without my supper, and my breakfast this morning was only a small piece of bread.'

'We haven't had any new clothes for months,' said Peggy. 'My shoes are dreadful. And I don't know what we shall do when the winter comes, because none of our coats will fit us.'

'You are much worse off than I am,' said Jack. 'I have never had anything nice, so I don't miss it. But you have had everything you wanted, and now it is all taken away from you – you haven't even a father and mother you can go to for help.'

'Do you remember *your* father and mother, Jack?' asked Mike. 'Did you always live with your old grandfather?'

'I never remember anyone except him,' said Jack. 'He's talking of going to live with an aunt of mine. If he does I shall be left all alone, for she won't have me, too.'

'Oh, Jack! Whatever will you do?' asked Nora.

'I shall be all right!' said Jack. 'The thing is what are *you* three going to do? I hate to see you all unhappy. If only we could all run away together!'

'We should be found at once and brought back,' said Mike gloomily. 'I know that. I've read in the papers about boys and girls running away, and they are always found by the police and brought back. If I knew some place where we would never be found, I *would* run away – and take the two girls with me too. I hate to see them bullied and worked so hard by Aunt Harriet.'

'Now listen to me,' said Jack suddenly, in such an earnest voice that all three children turned to him at once. 'If I tell you a very great secret will you promise never to say a word about it to anyone?'

'Oh, yes, Jack, we promise,' said all three.

'You can trust us, Jack,' said Mike.

'I know I can,' he said. 'Well, listen. I know a place where nobody could find us – if we ran away!'

'Where is it, Jack?' they all cried in great excitement.

'I'll show you this evening,' said Jack, getting up. 'Be by the lakeside at eight o'clock, when all your work is done, and I'll meet you there. I must go now, or Grandpa will be angry with me, and perhaps lock me into my room so that I can't get out again today.'

'Goodbye, Jack,' said Nora, who was feeling much better now. 'We'll see you this evening.'

Jack ran off, and the three children made their way slowly back to Uncle Henry's farm. They had taken their dinner out into the fields to eat – now they had to go back to work. Nora had a great deal of ironing to do, and Peggy had to clean the kitchen. It was a big stone kitchen, and Peggy knew it would take her until suppertime – and, oh dear, how tired she would be then! Aunt Harriet would scold her all the time, she knew.

'I've got to go and clean out the barn,' said Mike to the girls, 'but I'll be in at suppertime, and afterwards we'll see about this great secret of Jack's.'

They each began their work, but all the time they were thinking excitedly of the evening. What was Jack's secret? Where was the place he knew of? Could they really and truly run away?

They all got into trouble because they were thinking so hard of the evening that they did not do their work to Aunt Harriet's liking nor to Uncle Henry's either. Nora got shouted at again, and Peggy was in such trouble she cried bitterly for hours. She was made to scrub the kitchen floor all over again, and this made her late for supper.

Mike was shouted at by Uncle Henry for spilling some corn in the barn. The little boy said nothing, but he made up his mind that if it was possible to run away in safety he would do so, and take the girls with him, too.

'Nora and Peggy ought to be going to school and wearing nice clothes that fit them, and having friends to tea,' said Mike to himself. 'This is no life for them. They are just very hard-worked servants for Aunt Harriet, and she pays them nothing.'

The children ate their supper of bread and cheese in silence. They were afraid of speaking in case their aunt and uncle shouted at them. When they had finished Mike spoke to his aunt.

'Please may we go for a walk in the fields before we go to bed?' he asked.

'No, you can't,' said Aunt Harriet in her sharp voice. 'You'll just go to bed, all of you. There's a lot of work to do tomorrow, and I want you up early.'

The children looked at one another in dismay. But they had to do as they were told. They went upstairs to the big bedroom they all shared. Mike had a small bed in the corner behind a screen, and the two girls had a bigger bed between them.

'I believe Aunt Harriet and Uncle Henry are going out tonight, and that's why they want us to go to bed early,' said Mike. 'Well, if they do go out, we'll slip down and meet Jack by the river.'

'We won't get undressed then,' said Nora. 'We'll just slip under the sheets, dressed – and then it won't take us long to run down to the lake.'

The three children listened hard. They heard the front door close. Mike popped out of bed and ran to the front room. From there he could see the path to the gate. He saw his uncle and aunt walk down it, dressed to go out.

He ran back to the others. 'We'll wait for five minutes,' he said, 'then we'll go.'

They waited quietly. Then they all slipped downstairs and out of the back door. They ran down to the lake as fast as they could. Jack was there waiting for them.

'Hello, Jack,' said Mike. 'Here we are at last. They sent us to bed, but when they went out we slipped down here to meet you.'

'What's your great secret, Jack?' asked Nora, 'we are longing to know.'

'Well, listen,' said Jack. 'You know what a big lake this is, don't you, perfectly wild all round, except at the two ends where there are a few farmhouses and cottages. Now I know a little island, a good way up the south side of the lake, that I'm sure nobody knows at all. I don't think anyone but me has ever been there. It's a fine island, and would make the best hiding place in the world!'

The three children listened, their eyes wide with astonishment. An island on the big lake! Oh, if only they could really go there and hide – and live by themselves – with no unkind aunt and uncle to slap them and scold them and make them work hard all day long!

'Are you too tired to walk down the lakeside to a place where you can see the island?' asked Jack. 'I only found it quite by chance one day. The woods come right down to the lakeside opposite the island, and they are so thick that I don't think anyone has ever been through them, and so no one can have seen my island!'

'Jack! Jack! Take us to see your secret island!' begged Nora. 'Oh, we must go. We're all tired – but we must, must see the secret island.'

'Come on, then,' said Jack, pleased to see how excited the others were. 'Follow me. It's a good way.'

The barefooted boy took the three children across the fields to a wood. He threaded his way through the trees as if he were a rabbit. The wood thinned out and changed to a common, which, in turn, gave way to another wood, but this time the trees were so thick that it seemed as if there was no way through them at all.

But Jack kept on. He knew the way. He led the children without stopping, and at last they caught sight of the gleam of water. They had come back to the lakeside again. The evening was dim. The sun had sunk long since, and the children could hardly see.

Jack pushed his way through the trees that grew down to the waterside. He stood there and pointed silently to something. The children crowded round him.

'My secret island!' said Jack.

And so it was. The little island seemed to float on the dark lake-waters. Trees grew on it, and a little hill rose in the middle of it. It was a mysterious island, lonely and beautiful. All the children stood and gazed at it, loving it and longing to go to it. It looked so secret – almost magic.

'Well,' said Jack at last. 'What do you think? Shall we run away, and live on the secret island?'

'Yes!' whispered all the children. 'Let's!'

CHAPTER TWO

An Exciting Day

THE THREE children thought of nothing else but Jack's secret island all the next day. Could they possibly run away and hide there? Could they live there? How could they get food? What would happen if people came to look for them? Would they be found? How busy their minds were, thinking, thinking, planning, planning! Oh, the excitement of that secret island! It seemed so mysterious and lovely. If only, only they were all there, safe from all the shouting and unhappiness!

The first time the children had a little time together to talk, they spoke about the island.

'Mike, we *must* go!' said Nora.

'Mike, let's tell Jack we'll go,' said Peggy.

Mike scratched his curly black head. He felt old and worried. He wanted to go very badly – but would the three of them really be able to stand a wild life like that? No proper beds to sleep in – perhaps no proper food to eat – and suppose one of them was ill? Well, they would have to chance all that. They could always come back if things went too wrong.

'We'll go,' said Mike. 'We'll plan it all with Jack. He knows better than we do.'

So that night, when they met Jack, the four of them laid their plans. Their faces were red with excitement, their eyes were shining. An adventure! A real proper adventure, almost like Robinson Crusoe – for they were going to live all by themselves on a lonely island.

'We must be careful in our plans,' said Jack. 'We mustn't forget a single thing, for we ought not to go back to get anything, you know, or we might be caught.'

'Could we go over to the island and just see what it's like before we go to live there?' asked Nora. 'I would so love to see it.'

'Yes,' said Jack. 'We'll go on Sunday.'

'How can we go?' asked Mike. 'Do we have to swim?'

'No,' said Jack. 'I have an old boat. It was one that had been left to fall to pieces, and I found it and patched it up. It still gets water in, but we can bail that out. I'll take you over in that.'

The children could hardly wait for Sunday to come. They had to do a certain amount of work on Sundays, but usually they were allowed to take their dinner out and have a picnic afterwards.

It was June. The days were long and sunny. The farm

garden was full of peas, broad beans, gooseberries, and ripening cherries. The children stole into it and picked as many pea pods as they could find, and pulled up two big lettuces. Aunt Harriet gave them so little to eat that they always had to take something else as well. Mike said it wasn't stealing, because if Aunt Harriet had given them the food they earned by the hard work they did, they would have twice as much. They were only taking what they had earned. They had a loaf of bread between them, some butter, and some slices of ham, as well as the peas and lettuces. Mike pulled up some carrots, too. He said they would taste most delicious with the ham.

They hurried off to meet Jack. He was by the lakeside, carrying a bag on his back. He had his dinner in it. He showed them some fine red cherries, and a round cake.

'Mrs Lane gave me those for hoeing her garden yesterday,' he said. 'We'll have a fine dinner between us.'

'Where's the boat, Jack?' said Nora.

'You wait and see!' said Jack. 'I don't leave my secret things out for everyone to see! No one else but you three knows about my boat!'

He set off in the hot June sunshine, and the three children followed him. He kept close to the lakeside and although the children kept a sharp look-out for the boat they did not see it until Jack stopped and showed it to them.

'See that great alder bush hanging over the lake just there?' he said. 'Well, my boat's underneath it! It's well hidden, isn't it?'

Mike's eyes shone. He loved boats. He did hope Jack would let him help to row. The children pulled out the boat from under the thick tree. It was quite a big one, but very, very old. It had a good deal of water in, and Jack set everyone to work bailing it out. There was an old pair of oars in the boat, and Jack put them in place.

'Now get in,' he said. 'I've a good way to row. Would you like to take an oar, Mike?'

Of course Mike would! The two boys rowed over the water. The sun shone down hotly, but there was a little breeze that blew every now and again. Soon the children saw the secret island in the distance. They knew it because of the little hill it had in the middle.

The secret island had looked mysterious enough on the night they had seen it before – but now, swimming in the hot June haze, it seemed more enchanting than ever. As they drew near to it, and saw the willow trees that bent over the water's edge and heard the sharp call of moorhens that scuttled off, the children gazed in delight. Nothing but trees and birds and little wild animals. Oh, what a secret island, all for their very own, to live on and play on.

'Here's the landing place,' said Jack, and he guided

the boat to a sloping sandy beach. He pulled it up on the sand, and the children jumped out and looked round. The landing place was a natural little cove – a lovely spot for a picnic – but picnickers never came here! Only a lonely otter lay on the sand now and again, and moorhens scuttled across it. No fire had ever been made on this little beach to boil a kettle. No bits of old orange peel lay about, or rusty tins. It was quite unspoilt.

'Let's leave our things here and explore a bit,' said Mike, who was simply longing to see what the island was like. It seemed very big now they were on it.

'All right,' said Jack, and he put his bag down.

'Come on,' said Mike to the girls. 'This is the beginning of a big adventure.'

They left the little cove and went up through the thick trees. There were willows, alders, hazels, and elderberries at first, and then as they went up the hill that lay behind the cove there were silver birches and oaks. The hill was quite steep, and from the top the children could see a very long way – up the lake and down the lake.

'I say! If we come here to live, this hill will make an awfully good place to watch for enemies from here, all around!'

'Yes,' said Jack. 'Nobody would be able to take us by surprise.'

'We *must* come here, we must, we must!' said Nora. 'Oh, look at those rabbits, Peggy – they are as tame as can be, and that chaffinch nearly came on to my hand! Why are they so tame, Mike?'

'I suppose because they are not used to people,' said Mike. 'What's the other side of the hill, Jack? Shall we go down it?'

'There are caves on the other side of the hill,' said Jack. 'I haven't explored those. They would make good hiding places if anyone ever came to look for us here.'

They went down the hill on the other side. Gorse grew there and heather and bracken. Jack pointed out a big cave in the hillside. It looked dark and gloomy in the hot sunshine.

'We haven't time to go there now,' said Jack. 'But a cave would be an awfully good place to store anything in, wouldn't it? It would keep things nice and dry.'

A little way down the hill the children heard a bubbling noise.

'What's that?' asked Peggy, stopping.

'Look! It's a little spring!' cried Mike. 'Oh, Jack! This shall be our water supply! It's as cold as can be, and as clear as crystal!'

'It tastes fine, too,' said Jack. 'I had a drink last time I was here. Lower down, another spring joins this one, and there is a tiny brook.'

AN EXCITING DAY

At the bottom of the hill was a thick wood. In clear patches great bushes of brambles grew. Jack pointed them out.

'There will be thousands of blackberries in the autumn,' he said. 'And as for hazel nuts, you should see them! And in another place I know here, on a warm slope, you can find wild raspberries by the score!'

'Oh, do show us!' begged Mike. But Jack said there was not time. Besides, the raspberries wouldn't be ripe yet.

'The island is too big to explore all over today,' said Jack. 'You've seen most of it – this big hill with its caves, the springs, the thick wood, and beyond the wood is a grassy field and then the water again. Oh, it is a glorious place!'

'Jack, where shall we live on this island?' said Peggy, who always liked to have everything well settled in her mind.

'We shall build a house of wood,' said Jack. 'I know how to. That will do fine for the summer, and for the winter we will have to find a cave, I think.'

The children gazed at one another in glee. A house of wood, built by themselves – and a cave! How lucky they were to have a friend like Jack, who had a boat and a secret island!

They went back to the little landing place, hungry and happy. They sat down and ate their bread and ham, carrots and peas, cherries and lettuces, and cake. It was the loveliest meal they had ever had in their lives, they thought. A little moorhen walked up to them and seemed surprised to see so many people in its home. But it did not run away. It ran round, pecking at the lettuce leaves, saying, 'Fulluck, fulluck!' in its loud voice.

'If I could live here on this secret island always and always and always, and never grow up at all, I would be quite happy,' said Nora.

'Well, we'll have a shot at living here for a good while at least!' said Jack. 'Now, when shall we come?'

'And what shall we bring?' said Mike.

'Well, we don't really need a great deal at present,' said Jack. 'We can make soft beds of heather and bracken to lie on at night. What would be useful would be things like enamel mugs and plates and knives. I'll bring an axe and a very sharp woodman's knife. We'll need those when we build our house. Oh – and matches would be *most* useful for lighting fires. We shall have to cook our meals. I'll bring my fishing line along, too.'

The more the children talked about their plan, the more excited they got. At last they had arranged what to bring. They were gradually to hide things in a hollow tree by the lakeside, and then, when the time came, they could carry them to the boat and row off to the secret island, ready to set up house there.

'A frying pan would be useful,' said Nora.

'And a saucepan or two,' said Peggy, 'and a kettle. Oh! What fun it will be. I don't care how much we are shouted at now – I shall think of this exciting plan all day long!'

'We had better fix a day for starting off,' said Jack. 'What about a week from now? Sunday would be a good day for running away, because no one will come to look for us until night time, when we don't go home!'

'Yes! A week today!' cried everyone. 'Oooh! How happy we shall be!'

'Now we must go home,' said Jack, setting off to the boat. 'You can row if you like, Mike, and I'll bail out the water as we go. Get in, you girls.'

'Ay, ay, Captain!' they sang out, full of joy to think they had such a fine leader as Jack! Off they all went, floating across the water in the evening light. What would they be doing next Sunday?

CHAPTER THREE

The Escape

ALL THAT week the three children carried out their plans. Aunt Harriet and Uncle Henry could not understand what was different about the children – they did not seem to mind being scolded at all. Even Nora didn't burst into tears when she was shouted at. She was so happy when she thought of the secret island that she couldn't shed a tear!

The children took all the clothes they possessed down to the hollow tree by the lakeside. Mike took four enamel cups, some enamel plates, and two enamel dishes. Nora smuggled down an old kettle that Aunt Harriet had put away in a cupboard. She did not dare to take one of those on the stove. Peggy took a frying pan and a saucepan to the hollow tree, and had to put up with a dreadful scolding when her aunt could not find them.

Jack took a saucepan too, and an axe and a fine sharp knife. He also took some small knives and forks and spoons, for the other children did not dare to take these. There were only just enough put out for them and their

20

aunt and uncle to use. So they were glad when Jack found some and brought them along.

'Can you get some empty tins to store things in?' asked Jack. 'I am trying to get sugar and things like that, because we must have those, you know. Grandad gave me some money the other day, and I'm buying a few things to store.'

'Yes, I'll get some empty tins,' said Mike. 'Uncle has plenty in the shed. I can wash them out and dry them. And could you get matches, Jack? Aunt only leaves one box out, and that won't go far.'

'Well, I've got a small magnifying glass,' said Jack, and he showed it to the others. 'Look, if I focus the rays of the sun on to that bit of paper over there, see what happens. It burns it, and, hey presto, there's a fire ready-made!'

'Oh, good!' said Mike. 'We'll use that on a sunny day, Jack, and save our matches!'

'I'm bringing my workbasket in case we need to sew anything,' said Peggy.

'And I've got a box of mixed nails and an old hammer,' said Mike. 'I found them in the shed.'

'We're getting on!' said Jack, grinning, 'I say – what a time we're going to have!'

'I wish Sunday would come!' sighed Nora.

'I shall bring our snap cards and our game of ludo and

our dominoes,' said Peggy. 'We shall want to play games sometimes. And what about some books?'

'Good for you!' cried Mike. 'Yes – books and papers we'll have, too – we shall love to read quietly sometimes.'

The old hollow tree by the lakeside was soon full of the strangest collection of things. Not a day went by without something being added to it. One day it was a plank of wood. Another day it was half a sack of potatoes. Another day it was an old and ragged rug. Really, it was a marvel that the tree held everything!

At last Sunday came. The children were up long before their uncle and aunt. They crept into the kitchen garden and picked a basket of peas, pulled up six lettuces, added as many ripe broad beans as they could find, a bunch of young carrots, some radishes, and, putting their hands into the nest boxes of the hens, they found six new-laid eggs!

Nora crept indoors and went to the larder. What could she take that Aunt Harriet would not notice that morning? Some tea? Yes! A tin of cocoa from the top shelf. A packet of currants and a tin of rice from the store shelf, too. A big loaf, a few cakes from the cake tin! The little girl stuffed them all into her basket and raced out to join the others. Long before Aunt Harriet was up all these things were safely in the hollow tree.

THE ESCAPE

Peggy didn't quite like taking anything from the larder, but Mike said that as Aunt and Uncle wouldn't have to keep them after that day, they could quite well spare a few odds and ends for them.

'Anyway, if they paid us properly for our work, we would have enough to buy all these things and more,' he said, as he stuffed them into the tree.

They went back to the farm for the last time, to breakfast. Peggy cooked the breakfast, and hoped Aunt would not notice that her long iron cooking spoon was gone. She also hoped that Aunt would not want to get another candle from the packet in the larder, for Peggy knew Mike had taken the rest of them, and had taken an old lantern of Uncle's, too!

The children ate their breakfast in silence.

Aunt Harriet looked at them. 'I suppose you think you are going off for a picnic today!' she said. 'Well, you are not! You can stay and weed the kitchen garden, Peggy and Nora. And I've no doubt Uncle Henry can set Mike something to do. *Someone* has been taking cakes out of my tin, and so you'll all stay in today!'

The hearts of the three children sank. Today of all days! As soon as the girls were washing up alone in the scullery, Mike looked in at the window.

'You girls slip off down to the lake as soon as you get a

chance,' he said. 'Wait there for me. I won't be long!'

Peggy and Nora felt happier. They were to escape after all, then! They washed up a few more things and then saw their aunt going upstairs.

'She has gone to look out Uncle's Sunday suit and shirt,' whispered Nora. 'Quick! Now's our chance. We can slip out of the back door.'

Peggy ran to the cupboard under the dresser and took out a long bar of soap. 'We forgot all about soap!' she said. 'We shall want some! I just remembered in time!'

Nora looked round for something to take, too. She saw a great slab of margarine on the dresser, and she caught it up.

'This will help us in our frying!' she said. 'Come on, Peggy – we've no time to lose.'

They raced out of the back door, down the path, and out into the fields. In five minutes' time they were by the hollow tree, well out of sight. Jack was not yet there. They did not know how long Mike would be. He would not find it so easy to get away!

But Mike had laid his plans. He waited for the moment when his aunt discovered that the girls had gone, and then walked into the kitchen.

'What's the matter, Aunt Harriet?' he asked, pretending to be very much surprised at her angry face and voice.

'Where have those two girls gone?' cried his aunt.

'I expect they have only gone to get in the clothes or something,' said Mike. 'Shall I go and find them for you?'

'Yes, and tell them they'll get into big trouble for running off without finishing their work,' said his aunt in a rage.

Mike ran off, calling to his uncle that he was on an errand for his aunt. So Uncle Henry said nothing, but let him go. Mike tore across the fields to the lakeside and met the two girls there. They hugged one another in joy.

'Now, where's Jack?' said Mike. 'He said he would meet us as soon as he could.'

'There he is!' said Nora, and sure enough, there was Jack coming across the field, waving to them. He carried a heavy bag into which he had crammed all sorts of things at the very last moment – rope, an old mackintosh, two books, some newspapers, and other things. His face was shining with excitement.

'Good! You're here!' he said.

'Yes, but we nearly couldn't come,' said Nora, and she told Jack what had happened.

'I say! I hope this won't mean that your uncle and aunt will start to look for you too soon,' said Jack.

'Oh, no!' said Mike. 'It only means that they will make up their minds to punish us well when we get back this evening, but we shan't go back! They'll think we've gone off on our usual Sunday picnic.'

'Now we've got a lot to do,' said Jack seriously. 'This is all fun and excitement to us – but it's work, too – and we've got to get on with it. First, all these things must be carried from the hollow tree to the boat. Mike, you get out some of them and give them to the girls. Then we'll take the heavier things. I expect we shall have to come back to the tree three or four times before it's emptied.'

The four of them set off happily, carrying as much as they could. The sun was hot, and they puffed and panted, but who cared? They were off to the secret island at last!

It was a good walk to the boat, and they had to make four journeys altogether, carrying things carefully. At last there was nothing left in the hollow tree. They need not come back again.

'I'm jolly glad,' said Mike. 'Every time I get back to that hollow tree I expect to find Aunt or Uncle hidden inside it, ready to pop out at us!'

'Don't say such horrid things,' said Nora. 'We're leaving Aunt and Uncle behind for ever!'

They were at the boat, and were stowing things there as well as they could. It was a good thing the boat was fairly big or it would never have taken everything. The children had had to bail out a good deal of water before they could put anything in the bottom. It leaked badly, but as long as someone could bail out with a tin it was all right.

'Now then,' said Jack, looking round at the shore to see that nothing was left behind, 'are we ready?'

'Ay, ay, Captain!' roared the other three. 'Push off!'

The boat was pushed off. Mike and Jack took an oar each, for the boat was heavy and needed two people to pull it. It floated easily out on to the deeper water.

'We're off at last!' said Nora, in a little happy voice that sounded almost as if she were going to cry.

Nobody said anything more. The boat floated on and on, as Mike and Jack rowed strongly. Peggy bailed out the water that came in through the leaks. She wondered what it would be like not to sleep in a proper bed. She wondered what it would be like to wake up under the blue sky – to have no one to make her do this, that and the other. How happy she felt!

It was a long way to the island. The sun rose higher and higher. The adventurers felt hotter and hotter. At last Nora pointed excitedly in front.

'The secret island!' she cried. 'The secret island.'

Mike and Jack stopped rowing for a moment and the boat floated on slowly by itself whilst the four gazed at the lonely little island, hidden so well on the heart of the lake.

Their own island! It had no name. It was just the Secret Island!

Mike and Jack rowed on again. They came to the little sandy cove beneath the willow trees. Jack jumped out and pulled the boat in. The others jumped out too and gazed round.

'We're really here, we're really here, we're really here!' squealed Nora, jumping up and down and round and round in delight. 'We've escaped. We've come to live on this dear little hidden island.'

'Come on, Nora, give a hand,' ordered Jack. 'We've a lot to do before night, you know!'

Nora ran to help. The boat had to be unloaded, and that was quite a job. All the things were put on the beach under the willow trees for the time being. By the time that was finished the children were hotter than ever and very hungry and thirsty.

'Oh, for a drink!' groaned Mike.

'Peggy, do you remember the way to the spring?' asked Jack. 'You do? Well, just go and fill this kettle with water, will you? We'll all have a drink and something to eat!'

Peggy ran off up the hill and down the other side to the spring. She filled the kettle and went back. The others had put out enamel mugs ready to drink from. Mike was busy looking out something to eat, too. He had put out a loaf of bread, some young carrots, which they all loved to nibble, a piece of cheese each, and a cake.

What a meal that was! How they laughed and giggled and chattered! Then they lay back in the sun and shut their eyes. They were tired with all their hard work. One by one they fell asleep.

Jack awoke first. He sat up. 'Hey!' he said. 'This won't do! We've got to get our beds for the night and arrange a good sleeping place! We've dozens of things to do! Come on, everyone, to work, to work!'

But who minded work when it was in such a pleasant place? Peggy and Nora washed up the mugs and dishes in the lake water and set them in the sun to dry. The boys put all the stores in a good place and covered them with the old mackintosh in case it should rain. Tomorrow they would start to build their house.

'Now to get a sleeping place and bedding,' said Jack. 'Won't it be fun to sleep for the first time on the Secret Island!'

CHAPTER FOUR

The First Night on the Island

'WHERE DO you think would be the best place to sleep?' said Peggy, looking round the little cove.

'Well,' said Jack, 'I think it would be best to sleep under some thick trees somewhere, then, if it rains tonight, we shall not get too wet. But I don't think it will rain; the weather is quite settled.'

'There are two nice, big, thick oak trees just beyond the cove,' said Mike, pointing. 'Shall we find a place there?'

'Yes,' said Jack. 'Find a bramble bush or gorse bush near them to keep any wind off. Let's go and see what we think.'

They all went to the two big oak trees. Their branches swung almost down to the ground in places. Below grew clumps of soft heather, springy as a mattress. To the north was a great growth of gorse, thick and prickly.

'This looks a fine place to sleep,' said Jack. 'Look. Do you see this little place here, almost surrounded by gorse, and carpeted with heather? The girls could sleep here, and we could sleep just outside their cosy spot, to protect them. The oak trees would shelter us nicely overhead.'

THE FIRST NIGHT ON THE ISLAND

'Oh, I do think this is fine; I do, I do!' cried Nora, thinking that their green, heathery bedroom was the nicest in the world. She lay down on the heather. 'It is as soft as can be!' she said, 'and oh! there is something making a most delicious smell. What is it?'

'It is a patch of wild thyme,' said Jack. 'Look, there is a bit in the middle of the heather. You will smell it when you go to sleep, Nora!'

'All the same, Jack, the heather won't feel quite so soft when we have lain on it a few hours,' said Mike. 'We'd better get some armfuls of bracken too, hadn't we?'

'Yes,' said Jack. 'Come on up the hill. There is plenty of bracken there, and heaps of heather too. We will pick the bracken there, and put it in the sun to dry. The heather doesn't need drying. Pick plenty, for the softer we lie the better we'll sleep! Heyho for a starry night and a heathery bed!'

The four children gathered armfuls of bracken and put it out in the sun to wither and dry. The heather they carried back to their green bedroom under the oak tree. They spread it thickly there. It looked most deliciously soft! The thick gorse bushes kept off the breeze, and the oaks above waved their branches and whispered. What fun it all was!

'Well, there are our bedrooms ready,' said Jack. 'Now,

31

we'd better find a place to put our stores in. We won't be too far from the water, because it's so useful for washing ourselves and our dishes in.'

The children were hungry again. They got out the rest of the cakes, and finished up the bread, eating some peas with it, which they shelled as they ate.

'Are we going to have any supper?' asked Mike.

'We might have a cup of cocoa each and a piece of my cake,' said Jack. 'We must be careful not to eat everything at once that we've brought, or we'll go short! I'll do some fishing tomorrow.'

'Shall we begin to build the house tomorrow?' asked Mike, who was longing to see how Jack meant to make their house.

'Yes,' said Jack. 'Now you two girls wash up the mugs again, and Mike and I will find a good place for the stores.'

The girls went to the water and washed the things. The boys wandered up the beach – and, at the back of the sandy cove, they found just the very place they wanted!

There was a sandy bank there, with a few old willows growing on top of it, their branches drooping down. Rain had worn away the sandy soil from their roots, and underneath there was a sort of shallow cave, with roots running across it here and there.

'Look at that!' said Jack in delight. 'Just the place we

want for our stores! Nora, Peggy, come and look here!'

The girls came running. 'Oh,' said Peggy, pleased, 'we can use those big roots as shelves, and stand our tins and cups and dishes on them! Oh, it's a proper little larder!'

'Well, if you girls get the stores from the cove and arrange them neatly here,' said Jack. 'Mike and I will go and fill the kettle from the spring, and we'll see if there isn't a nearer spring, because it's a long way up the hill and down the other side.'

'Can't we come with you?' asked Peggy.

'No, you arrange everything,' said Jack. 'It had better all be done as quickly as possible, because you never know when it's going to turn wet. We don't want our stores spoilt.'

Leaving Peggy and Nora to arrange the tins, baskets, and odds and ends neatly in the root-larder, the two boys went up the hill behind the cove. They separated to look for a spring, and Mike found one! It was a very tiny one, gushing out from under a small rock, and it ran down the hill like a little waterfall, getting lost in the heather and grass here and there. Its way could be seen by the rushes that sprang up beside its course.

'I expect it runs down into the lake,' said Mike. 'It's a very small spring, but we can use it to fill our kettle, and it won't take us quite so long as going to the other spring.

If we have to live in the caves during the winter, the other spring will be more useful then, for it will be quite near the cave.'

They filled the kettle. It was lovely up there on the hillside in the June sun. Bees hummed and butterflies flew all round. Birds sang, and two or three moorhens cried 'Fulluck, fulluck!' from the water below.

'Let's go to the top of the hill and see if we can spy anyone coming up or down the lake,' said Jack. So they went right up to the top, but not a sign of anyone could they see. The waters of the lake were calm and clear and blue. Not a boat was on it. The children might have been quite alone in the world.

They went down to the girls with the full kettle. Nora and Peggy proudly showed the boys how they had arranged the stores. They had used the big roots for shelves, and the bottom of the little cave they had used for odds and ends such as Jack's axe and knife, the hammer and nails, and so on.

'It's a nice dry place,' said Peggy. 'It's just right for a larder, and it's so nice and near the cove. Jack, where are we going to build our house?'

Jack took the girls and Mike to the west end of the cove, where there was a thicket of willows. He forced his way through them and showed the others a fine clear place right in the very middle of the trees.

'Here's the very place,' he said. 'No one would ever guess there was a house just here, if we built one! The willows grow so thickly that I don't suppose anyone but ourselves would ever know they could be got through.'

They talked about their house until they were tired out. They made their way back to the little beach and Jack said they would each have a cup of cocoa, a piece of cake, and go to bed!

He and Mike soon made a fire. There were plenty of dry twigs about, and bigger bits of wood. It did look cheerful to see the flames dancing. Jack could not use his little magnifying glass to set light to the paper or twigs because the sun was not bright enough then. It was sinking down in the west. He used a match. He set the kettle on the fire to boil.

'It would be better tomorrow to swing the kettle over the flames on a tripod of sticks,' he said. 'It will boil more quickly then.'

But nobody minded how slowly the kettle boiled. They lay on their backs in the sand, looking up at the evening sky, listening to the crackle of the wood, and smelling a mixture of wood-smoke and honeysuckle. At last the kettle sent out a spurt of steam, and began to hiss. It was boiling.

Nora made the cocoa, and handed it round in mugs. 'There's no milk,' she said. 'But there is some sugar.'

They munched their cake and drank their cocoa. Though it had no milk in it, it was the nicest they had ever tasted.

'I do like seeing the fire,' said Nora. 'Oh, Jack, why are you stamping it out?'

'Well,' said Jack, 'people may be looking for us tonight, you know, and a spire of smoke from this island would give our hiding place away nicely! Come on, now, everyone to bed! We've hard work to do tomorrow!'

Peggy hurriedly rinsed out the mugs. Then all of them went to their green, heathery bedroom. The sun was gone. Twilight was stealing over the secret island.

'Our first night here!' said Mike, standing up and looking down on the quiet waters of the lake. 'We are all alone, the four of us, without a roof over our heads even, but I'm so happy!'

'So am I!' said everyone. The girls went to their hidden green room in the gorse and lay down in their clothes. It seemed silly to undress when they were sleeping out of doors. Mike threw them the old ragged rug.

'Throw that over yourselves,' he said. 'It may be cold tonight, sleeping out for the first time. You won't be frightened, will you?'

'No,' said Peggy. 'You two boys will be near, and, anyway, what is there to be frightened of?'

They lay down on the soft heather, and pulled the old rug over them. The springy heather was softer than the old hard bed the two girls had been used to at home. The little girls put their arms round one another and shut their eyes. They were fast asleep almost at once.

But the boys did not sleep so quickly. They lay on their heathery beds and listened to all the sounds of the night. They heard the little grunt of a hedgehog going by. They saw the flicker of bats overhead. They smelt the drifting scent of honeysuckle, and the delicious smell of wild thyme crushed under their bodies. A reed warbler sang a beautiful little song in the reeds below, and then another answered.

'Is that a blackbird?' asked Mike.

'No, a reed warbler,' said Jack. 'They sing as beautifully as any bird that sings in the daytime! Listen, do you hear that owl?'

'Oooo-ooo-ooo-oooo!' came a long, quivering sound; 'ooo-ooo-ooo-ooo!'

'He's hunting for rats and voles,' said Jack. 'I say, look at the stars, Mike.'

'Don't they seem far away,' said Mike, looking up into the purple night sky, which was set with thousands of bright stars. 'I say, Jack, it's awfully nice of you to come away with us like this and share your secret island.'

'It isn't nice of me at all,' said Jack. 'I wanted to. I'm doing just exactly what I most want to do. I only hope we shan't be found and taken back, but I'll take jolly good care no one finds us! I'm laying my plans already!'

But Mike was not listening. His eyes shut, he forgot the owls and the stars; he fell asleep and dreamt of building a house with Jack, a lovely house.

Jack fell asleep, too. And soon the rabbits that lived under their gorse bush came slyly out and peeped at the sleeping children in surprise. Who were they?

But, as the children did not move, the rabbits grew bold and went out to play just as usual. Even when one ran over Mike by mistake, the little boy did not know it. He was *much* too fast asleep!

CHAPTER FIVE

The Building of the House

WHAT FUN it was to wake up that first morning on the island! Jack awoke first. He heard a thrush singing so loudly on a tree near by that he woke up with a jump.

'Mind how you do it,' said the thrush, 'mind how you do it!'

Jack grinned. 'I'll mind how I do it all right!' he said to the singing thrush. 'Hi, Mike! Wake up! The sun is quite high!'

Mike woke and sat up. At first he didn't remember where he was. Then a broad smile came over his face. Of course – they were all on the secret island! How perfectly glorious!

'Peggy, Nora! Get up!' he cried. The girls awoke and sat up in a hurry. Wherever were they? What was this green bedroom – oh, of course, it was their heathery bedroom on the secret island!

Soon all four children were up and about. Jack made them take off their things and have a dip in the lake. It was simply lovely, but the water felt cold at first. When

39

they had dried themselves on an old sack – for they had no towels – the children felt terribly hungry. But Jack had been busy. He had set his fishing line, and, even as they bathed, he had seen the float jerk up and down. It was not long before Jack proudly laid four fine trout on the sand of the cove, and set about to make a fire to cook them.

Mike went to fill the kettle to make some tea. Peggy got some big potatoes out of the sack and put them almost in the fire to cook in their skins. Jack found the frying pan in their storeroom and put a piece of margarine in to fry the fish, which he knew exactly how to clean.

'I don't know what we should do without you,' said Mike, as he watched Jack. 'Goodness! How I shall enjoy my breakfast!'

They all did. The tea did not taste very nice without milk. 'It's a pity we can't get milk,' said Jack. 'We shall miss that, I'm afraid. Now let's all wash up, and put everything away – and then we'll start on our house!'

In great excitement everything was washed up and put away. Then Jack led the way through the thick willow trees, and they came to the little clear place in the centre of them.

'Now, this is how I mean to build the house,' he said. 'Do you see these little willow trees here – one there

– one there – two there – and two there. Well, I think you will find that if we climb up and bend down the top branches, they will meet each other nicely in the centre, and we can weave them into one another. That will make the beginning of a roof. With my axe I shall chop down some other young willow trees, and use the trunk and thicker branches for walls. We can drive the trunks and branches into the ground between the six willow trees we are using, and fill up any cracks with smaller branches woven across. Then if we stuff every corner and crevice with bracken and heather, we shall have a fine big house, with a splendid roof, windproof and rainproof. What do you think of that?'

The other children listened in the greatest excitement. It sounded too good to be true. Could it be as easy as all that?

'Jack, can we really do it?' said Mike. 'It sounds all right – and those willow trees are just the right distance from one another to make a good big house – and their top branches will certainly overlap well.'

'Oh, let's begin, let's begin!' cried Nora, impatient as usual, dancing up and down.

'I'll climb up this first willow tree and swing the branches over with my weight,' said Jack. 'All you others must catch hold of them and hold them till I slip down.

Then I'll climb another tree and bend those branches over too. We'll tie them together, and then I'll climb up the other trees. Once we've got all the top branches bending down touching one another, and overlapping nicely, we can cut long willow-sticks and lace our roof together. I'll show you how to.'

Jack swung himself up into one of the little willow trees. It was only a young one, with a small trunk – but it had a head of long, fine branches, easy to bend. Jack swung them down, and the girls and Mike caught them easily. They held on to them whilst Jack slid down the tree and climbed another. He did the same thing there, bending down the supple branches until they reached and rested on top of those bent down from the other tree.

'Tie them together, Mike!' shouted Jack. 'Peggy, go and find the rope I brought.'

Peggy darted off. She soon came back with the rope. Mike twisted it round the branches of the two trees, and tied them firmly together.

'It's beginning to look like a roof already!' shouted Nora, in excitement. 'Oh, I want to sit underneath it!'

She sat down under the roof of willow boughs, but Jack called to her.

'Get up, Nora! You've got to help! I'm up the third tree now – look, here come the top branches bending over with my weight – catch them and hold them!'

Nora and Peggy caught them and held on tightly. The branches reached the others and overlapped them. Mike was soon busy tying them down, too.

The whole morning was spent in this way. By dinnertime all the six trees had been carefully bent over. Jack showed Mike and the girls how to weave the branches together, so that they held one another and made a fine close roof. 'You see, if we use the trees like this, their leaves will still grow and will make a fine thick roof,' said Jack. 'Now, although our house has no walls as yet, we at least have a fine roof to shelter under if it rains!'

'I want something to eat,' said Nora. 'I'm so hungry that I feel I could eat snails!'

'Well, get out four eggs, and we'll have some with potatoes,' said Jack. 'We'll boil the eggs in our saucepan. There's plenty of potatoes, too. After the eggs are boiled we'll boil some potatoes and mash them up. That will be nice for a change. We'll nibble a few carrots, too, and have some of those cherries.'

'We do have funny meals,' said Peggy, going to get the saucepan and the eggs, 'but I do like them! Come on, Nora, help me get the potatoes and peel them whilst the eggs are boiling. And Mike, get some water, will you? We haven't enough.'

Soon the fire was burning merrily and the eggs were boiling in the saucepan. The girls peeled the potatoes, and Jack washed the carrots. He went to get some water to drink, too, for everyone was very thirsty.

'You'd better catch some more fish for tonight, Jack,' said Peggy. 'I hope our stores are going to last out a bit! We do seem to eat a lot!'

'I've been thinking about that,' said Jack, watching the potatoes boiling. 'I think I'll have to row to land occasionally and get more food. I can get it from Grandad's farm. There are plenty of potatoes there, and I can always get the eggs from the hen-house. Some of the hens are mine – and there's a cow that's really mine too, for Grandad gave her to me when she was a calf!'

'I wish we had hens and a cow here!' said Peggy. 'We should have lots of milk then and plenty of eggs!'

'How would we get hens and a cow here?' said Mike, laughing. 'I think Jack's idea of rowing across to land sometimes is a good one. He can go at night. He knows the way, and could get back before day breaks.'

'It's dangerous, though,' said Peggy. 'Suppose he were caught? We couldn't do without Jack!'

The children ate their dinner hungrily. They thought that eggs and potatoes had never tasted so nice before. The sun shone down hotly. It was simply perfect weather.

Nora lay down when she had finished her meal and closed her eyes. She felt lazy and sleepy.

Jack poked her with his foot. 'You're not to go to sleep, Nora,' he said. 'We must get on with our house, now we've started. We've got to clear up as usual, and then we must get back to the house. We'll start on the walls this afternoon.'

'But I'm sleepy,' said Nora. She was rather a lazy little girl, and she thought it would be lovely to have a nap whilst the others got on with the work. But Jack was not the one to let anyone slack. He jerked Nora to her feet and gave her a push.

'Go on, lazybones,' he said. 'I'm captain here. Do as you're told.'

'I didn't know you were captain,' said Nora, rather sulkily.

'Well, you know now,' said Jack. 'What do the others say about it?'

'Yes, you're captain, Jack,' said Mike and Peggy together. 'Ay, ay, sir!'

Nobody said any more. They washed up in the lake and cleared the things away neatly. They put some more wood on the fire to keep it burning, because Jack said it was silly to keep on lighting it. Then they all ran off to the willow thicket.

45

Jack made himself busy. He chopped down some willow saplings – young willow trees – with his axe, and cut off the longer branches.

'We'll use these to drive into the ground for walls,' said Jack. 'Where's that old spade, Mike? Did you bring it as I said?'

'Yes, here it is,' said Mike. 'Shall I dig holes to drive the sapling trunks into?'

'Yes,' said Jack. 'Dig them fairly deep.'

So Mike dug hard in the hot sun, making holes for Jack to ram the willow wood into. The girls stripped the leaves off the chopped-down trees, and with Jack's knife cut off the smaller twigs. They trimmed up the bigger branches nicely.

Everyone worked hard until the sun began to go down. The house was not yet built – it would take some days to do that – but at any rate there was a fine roof, and part of the wall was up. The children could quite well see how the house would look when it was done – and certainly it would be big, and very strong. They felt proud of themselves.

'We'll do no more today,' said Jack. 'We are all tired. I'll go and see if there are any fish on my line.'

But, alas! there were no fish that night!

'There's some bread left and a packet of currants,'

said Peggy. 'And some lettuces and margarine. Shall we have those?'

'This food question is going to be a difficult one,' said Jack thoughtfully. 'We've plenty of water – we shall soon have a house – but we must have food or we shall starve. I shall catch rabbits, I think.'

'Oh, no, Jack, don't do that,' said Nora. 'I do like rabbits so much.'

'So do I, Nora,' said Jack. 'But if rabbits were not caught, the land would soon be overrun with them, you know. You have often had rabbit pie, haven't you? And I guess you liked it, too!'

'Yes, I did,' said Nora. 'Well, if you are sure you can catch them so that they are not hurt or in pain, Jack, I suppose you'll have to.'

'You leave it to me,' said Jack. 'I don't like hurting things any more than you do. But I know quite well how to skin rabbits. If it makes you feel squeamish, you two girls can leave it to Mike and me. So long as you can cook the rabbits for dinner, that's all you need worry about. And ever since Peggy said she wished we had a cow and some hens, I've been thinking about it. I believe we could manage to get them over here on to the island – then we *would* be all right!'

Mike, Peggy, and Nora stared at Jack in amazement.

What a surprising boy he was! However could they get a cow and hens?

'Let's hurry up and get the supper,' said Jack, smiling at their surprised faces. 'I'm hungry. We'll think about things tomorrow. We'll have our meal now and a quiet read afterwards, then to bed early. Tomorrow we'll go on with the house.'

Soon they were munching bread and margarine, and eating lettuce. They saved the currants for another time. Then they got out books and papers and sprawled on the soft heather, reading whilst the daylight lasted. Then they had a dip in the lake, threw on their clothes again, and settled down for the night in their heathery beds.

'Goodnight, everyone,' said Mike. But nobody answered – they were all asleep!

CHAPTER SIX

Willow House Is Finished

THE NEXT day, after a meal of fish and lettuce, the children were ready to go on with the building of their house in the willow thicket. It was lucky that Jack had caught more fish on his line that morning, for stores were getting low. There were still plenty of potatoes, but not much else. Jack made up his mind that he would have to take the boat and see what he could bring back in it that night. There was no doubt but that food was going to be their great difficulty.

All morning the four children worked hard at the house. Jack cut down enough young willows to make the walls. Mike dug the holes to drive in the willow stakes. He and Jack drove them deeply in, and the girls jumped for joy to see what fine straight walls of willow the boys were making.

The willow stakes were set a little way apart, and Jack showed the girls how to take thin, supple willow branches and weave them in and out of the stakes to hold the walls in place, and to fill up the gaps. It was quite easy to do this when they knew how, but they got very hot.

Mike went up and down to the spring a dozen times that morning to fetch water! They all drank pints of it, and were glad of its coldness. The sun was really very hot, though it was nice and shady in the green willow thicket.

'It begins to look like a house now,' said Jack, pleased. 'Look, this front gap here is where we shall have the door. We can make that later of long stakes interwoven with willow strips, and swing it on some sort of a hinge so that it opens and shuts. But we don't need a door at present.'

That day all the walls were finished, and the girls had gone a good way towards weaving the stakes together so that the walls stood firmly and looked nice and thick.

'In the olden days people used to fill up the gaps with clay and let it dry hard,' said Jack. 'But I don't think there's any clay on this island, so we must stuff up the cracks with dried bracken and heather. That will do nicely. And the willow stakes we have rammed into the ground will grow, and throw out leaves later on, making the wall thicker still.'

'How do you mean – the stakes we have cut will grow?' asked Mike in surprise. 'Sticks don't grow, surely!'

Jack grinned. 'Willow sticks do!' he said. 'You can cut a willow branch off the tree – strip it of all buds and leaves, and stick it in the ground, and you'll find that, although it has no roots, and no shoots – it will put out both and grow into a willow tree by itself! Willows are full of life, and you can't stamp it out of them!'

'Well – our house will be growing all the year round, then!' cried Nora. 'How funny!'

'I think it's lovely!' said Peggy. 'I like things to be as alive as that. I shall love to live in a house that's growing over me – putting out roots and shoots and buds and leaves! What shall we call our house, Jack?'

'Willow House!' said Jack. 'That's the best name for it!'

'It's a good name,' said Peggy. 'I like it. I like everything here. It's glorious. Just us four – and our secret island. It's the loveliest adventure that ever was!'

'If only we had more to eat!' said Mike, who seemed to feel hungry every hour of the day. 'That's the only thing I don't like about this adventure!'

'Yes,' said Jack. 'We'll have to put that right! Don't worry. We shall get over it somehow!'

That night there was nothing much to eat but potatoes. Jack said he would go off in the boat as soon as it was dark, to see what he could find at his old farm.

So he set off. He took with him a candle, set in the lantern, but he did not light it in case he should be seen.

'Wait up for me,' he said to the others, 'and keep a small fire going – not big, in case the glow could be seen.'

The other three waited patiently for Jack to come back. He seemed a long, long time. Nora stretched herself out on the old rug and fell asleep. But Mike and Peggy kept awake. They saw the moon come up and light everything. The secret island seemed mysterious again in the moonlight. Dark shadows stretched beneath the trees. The water lapped against the sand, black as night, close by them, but silvered where the moon caught it beyond. It was a warm night, and the children were hot, even though they had no covering.

It seemed hours before they heard the splash of oars. Mike ran down to the edge of the water and waited. He saw the boat coming softly over the water in the moonlight. He called Jack.

'Hello, there, Jack! Are you all right?'

'Yes,' said Jack's voice. 'I've got plenty of news too!'

The boat scraped on the sand and stones. Mike pulled it up the beach, and Jack jumped out.

'I've got something here for us!' said Jack, and they saw his white teeth in the moonlight as he grinned at them. Put your hands down there in the boat, Nora.'

Nora did – and squealed.

'There's something soft and warm and feathery there!' she said. 'What is it?'

'Six of my hens!' said Jack. 'I found them roosting in

52

the hedges! I caught them and trussed them up so that they couldn't move! My word, they were heavy to carry! But we shall have plenty of eggs now! They can't escape from the island!'

'Hurrah!' cried Peggy. 'We can have eggs for breakfast, dinner, and tea!'

'What else have you brought?' asked Mike.

'Corn for the hens,' said Jack. 'And packets of seeds of all kinds from the shed. And some tins of milk. And a loaf of bread, rather stale. And lots more vegetables!'

'And here are some cherries,' said Nora, pulling out handfuls of red cherries from the boat. 'Did you pick these, Jack?'

'Yes,' said Jack. 'They are from the tree in our garden. It's full of them now.'

'Did you see your grandfather?' asked Mike.

'Yes,' grinned Jack, 'But he didn't see me! He's going away – to live with my aunt. The farm is to be shut up, and someone is to feed the animals until it's sold. So I think I shall try and get my own cow somehow, and make her swim across the lake to the island!'

'Don't be silly, Jack,' said Peggy. 'You could never do that!'

'You don't know what I can do!' said Jack. 'Well, listen – I heard my Grandad talking to two friends of his, and everyone is wondering where we've all gone! They've searched everywhere for us – in all the nearby towns and villages, and in all the country round about!'

'Oooh!' said the three children, feeling rather frightened. 'Do you suppose they'll come here?'

'Well, they may,' said Jack. 'You never know. I've always been a bit afraid that the smoke from our fire will give the game away to someone. But don't let's worry about that till it happens.'

'Are the police looking for us, too?' asked Peggy.

'Oh yes,' said Jack. 'Everyone is, as far as I can make out. I heard Grandad tell how they've searched barns and stacks and ditches, and gone to every town for twenty miles round, thinking we might have run away on a lorry. They don't guess how near we are!'

'Is Aunt Harriet very upset?' asked Peggy.

'Very!' grinned Jack. 'She's got no one to wash and scrub and cook for her now! But that's all she cares, I expect! Well, it's good news about my Grandad going to live with my aunt. I can slip to and fro and not be seen by him now. My word, I wished you were with me when I got these hens. They did peck and scratch and flap about. I was afraid someone would hear them.'

'Where shall we put them?' said Mike, helping Jack to carry them up the beach.

WILLOW HOUSE IS FINISHED

'I vote we put them into Willow House till the morning,' said Jack. 'We can stop up the doorway with something.'

So they bundled the squawking hens into Willow House, and stopped up the doorway with sticks and bracken. The hens fled to a corner and squatted there, terrified. They made no more noise.

'I'm jolly tired,' said Jack. 'Let's have a few cherries and go to bed.'

They munched the ripe cherries, and then went to their green bedroom. The bracken which they had picked and put on the hillside to dry had been quite brown and withered by that afternoon, so the girls had added it to their bed and the boys', and tonight their beds seemed even softer and sweeter-smelling than usual. They were all tired. Mike and Jack talked for a little while, but the girls went to sleep quickly.

They slept late the next morning. Peggy woke first, and sat up, wondering what the unusual noise was that she heard. It was a loud cackling.

'Of course! The hens!' she thought. She slipped off her bracken-and-heather bed, jumped lightly over the two sleeping boys and ran to Willow House. She pulled aside the doorway and squeezed inside. The hens fled to a corner when they saw her, but Peggy saw a welcome sight!

Four of the hens had laid eggs! Goody! Now they

could have a fine breakfast! The little girl gathered them up quickly, then, stopping up the doorway again, she ran out. She soon had a fire going, and, when the others sat up, rubbing their eyes, Peggy called them.

'Come on! Breakfast! The hens have laid us an egg each!'

They ran to breakfast. 'We'll have a dip afterwards,' said Mike. 'I feel so hungry.'

'We must finish Willow House properly today,' said Jack. 'And we must decide what to do with the hens, too. They can't run loose till they know us and their new home. We must put up some sort of enclosure for them.'

After breakfast the four of them set to work to make a tiny yard for the hens. They used willow stakes again and quickly built a fine little fence, too high for the hens to jump over. Jack made them nesting places of bracken, and hoped they would lay their eggs there. He scattered some seed for them, and they pecked at it eagerly. Peggy gave them a dish of water.

'They will soon know this is their home and lay their eggs here,' said Jack. 'Now, come on, let's get on with Willow House! You two girls stuff up the cracks with heather and bracken, and Mike and I will make the door.'

Everyone worked hard. The girls found it rather a nice job to stuff the soft heather and bracken into the cracks and make the house rain and windproof. They were so happy in their job that they did not notice what a fine door Jack and Mike had made of woven willow twigs. The boys called the girls, and proudly showed them what they had done.

The door had even been fixed on some sort of a hinge, so that it swung open and shut! It looked fine! It did not quite fit at the top, but nobody minded that. It was a door – and could be shut or opened, just as they pleased. Willow House was very dark inside when the door was shut – but that made it all the more exciting!

'I'm so hungry and thirsty now that I believe I could eat all the food we've got!' said Mike at last.

'Yes, we really must have something to eat,' said Jack. 'We've got plenty of bread and potatoes and vegetables. Let's cook some broad beans. They are jolly good. Go and look at my fishing line, Mike, and see if there are any fish on it.'

There was a fine trout, and Mike brought it back to cook. Soon the smell of frying rose on the air, and the children sniffed hungrily. Fish, potatoes, bread, beans, cherries, and cocoa with milk from one of Jack's tins. What a meal!

'I'll think about getting Daisy the cow across next,' said Jack, drinking his cocoa. 'We simply must have milk.'

'And, Jack, we could store some of our things in Willow

House now, couldn't we?' said Peggy. 'The ants get into some of the things in the cave-larder. It's a good place for things like hammers and nails, but it would be better to keep our food in Willow House. Are we going to live in Willow House, Jack?'

'Well, we'll live in the open air mostly, I expect,' said Jack, 'but it will be a good place to sleep in when the nights are cold and rainy, and a good shelter on bad days. It's our sort of home.'

'It's a lovely home,' said Nora, 'the nicest there ever was! What fun it is to live like this!'

CHAPTER SEVEN

The Cow Comes to the Island

A DAY or two went by. The children were busy, for there seemed lots of things to do. The door of Willow House came off and had to be put on again more carefully. One of the hens escaped, and the four children spent nearly the whole morning looking for it. Jack found it at last under a gorse bush, where it had laid a big brown egg.

They made the fence of the hen-yard a bit higher, thinking that the hen had been able to jump over. But Mike found a hole in the fence through which he was sure the hen had squeezed, and very soon it was blocked up with fronds of bracken. The hens squawked and clucked, but they seemed to be settling down, and always ran eagerly to Nora when she fed them twice a day.

Mike thought it would be a good idea to make two rooms inside Willow House, instead of one big room. The front part could be a sort of living-room, with the larder in a corner, and the back part could be a bedroom, piled with heather and bracken to make soft lying. So they worked at a partition made of willow, and put it up to make two rooms. They left a doorway between, but did not make a door. It was nice to have a two-roomed house!

One evening Jack brought something unusual to the campfire on the little beach. Mike stared at what he was carrying.

'You've caught some rabbits!' he said, 'and you've skinned them, too, and got them ready for cooking!'

'Oh, Jack!' said Nora. 'Must you catch those dear little rabbits? I do love them so much, and it is such fun to watch them playing about round us in the evenings.'

'I know,' said Jack, 'but we must have meat to eat sometimes. Now, don't worry, Nora – they did not suffer any pain and you know you have often eaten rabbit pie at home.'

All the same, none of the children enjoyed cooking the rabbits, though they couldn't help being glad of a change of food. They were getting a little tired of fish. Nora said she felt as if she couldn't look a rabbit in the face that evening!

'In Australia, rabbits are as much of a pest as rats are here,' said Jack, who seemed to know all sorts of things. 'If we were in Australia we would think we had done a good deed to get rid of a few pests.'

'But we're not in Australia,' said Peggy. Nobody said any more, and the meal was finished in silence. The girls washed up as usual, and the boys went to get some water from the spring ready to boil in the morning. Then they all had a dip in the lake.

'I think I'll have a shot at getting my cow along tonight,' said Jack, as they dressed themselves again.

'You can't, Jack!' cried Nora. 'You'd never get a cow here!'

'I'll come with you, Jack,' said Mike. 'You'll want someone to help you.'

'Right!' said Jack. 'We'll start off as soon as it's dark.'

'Oh, Jack!' said the girls, excited to think of a cow coming. 'Where shall we keep it?'

'It had better live on the other side of the island,' said Jack. 'There is some nice grass there. It won't like to eat heather.'

'How will you bring it, Jack?' asked Mike. 'It will be difficult to get it into the boat, won't it?'

'We shan't get it into the boat, silly!' said Jack, laughing. 'We shall make it swim *behind* the boat!'

The other three stared at Jack in surprise. Then they began to laugh. It was funny to think of a cow swimming behind the boat to their secret island!

When it was dark, the two boys set off. The girls called goodbye, and then went to Willow House, for the evening was not quite so warm as usual. They lighted a candle and talked. It was fun to be on the secret island alone.

THE SECRET ISLAND

The boys rowed down the lake and came to the place where Jack usually landed – a well-hidden spot by the lakeside, where trees came right down to the water. They dragged the boat in and then made their way through the wood. After some time they came to the fields that lay round the house of Jack's grandfather. Jack looked at the old cottage. There was no light in it. No one was there. His grandfather had gone away. In the field nearby some cows and horses stood, and the boys could hear one of the horses saying, 'Hrrrumph! Hrrrrumph!'

'Do you see that shed over there, Mike?' said Jack, in a low voice. 'Well, there are some lengths of rope there. Go and get them whilst I try to find which is my own cow. The rope is in the corner, just by the door.'

Mike stumbled off over the dark field to the tumble down shed in the corner. Jack went among the cows, making a curious chirrupy noise. A big brown and white cow left the others and went lumbering towards Jack.

Jack cautiously struck a match and looked at it. It was Daisy, the cow he had brought up from a calf. He rubbed its soft nose, and called to Mike:

'Hurry up with that rope! I've got the cow.'

Mike had been feeling about in the shed for rope and had found a great coil of it. He stumbled over the field to Jack.

THE COW COMES TO THE ISLAND

'Good,' said Jack, making a halter for the patient animal. 'Now, before we go, I'd like to pop into the old cottage and see if I can find anything we'd be glad of.'

'Could you find some towels, do you think?' asked Mike. 'I do hate having to dry myself with old sacks.'

'Yes, I'll see if there are any left,' said Jack, and he set off quietly towards the old cottage. He found the door locked, but easily got in at a window. He struck a match and looked round. There were only two rooms in the cottage, a living-room and a bedroom. All the furniture had gone. Jack looked behind the kitchen door, and found what he had hoped to see – a big roller-towel still hanging there. It was very dirty, but could easily be washed. He looked behind the bedroom door – yes, there was a roller-towel there, too! Good! His grandfather hadn't thought of looking behind the doors and taking those when he went. Jack wondered if the old carpet left on the floor was worth taking, too, but he thought not. Good clean heather made a better carpet!

Jack wandered out to the little shed at the back of the cottage – and there he did indeed make a find! There was an old wooden box there, and in it had been put all the clothes he possessed! His grandfather had not thought it worth while to take those with him. There they were, rather ragged, it is true, but still, they were clothes! There were three shirts, a few vests, an odd pair of trousers, an overcoat, a pair of old shoes, and a ragged blanket!

Jack grinned. He would take all these back with him. They might be useful when the cold weather came. He thought the best way to take them back would be to wear them all – so the boy put on all the vests, the shirts, the trousers, the shoes, and the overcoat over his own clothes, and wrapped the blanket round him, too! What a strange sight he looked!

Then he went out to the garden and filled his many pockets with beans and peas and new potatoes. After that he thought it was time to go back to Mike and the cow. Mike would be tired of holding the animal by now!

So, carrying the two dirty towels, Jack made his way slowly over the field to Mike.

'I thought you were never coming!' said Mike, half-cross. 'Whatever happened to you? This cow is getting tired of standing here with me.'

'I found a lot of my clothes,' said Jack, 'and an old blanket and two towels. The cow will soon get some exercise! Come on! You carry the towels and this blanket, and I'll take Daisy.'

They went back over the fields and through the thick wood to the boat. The cow did not like it when they came to the wood. She could not see where they were going and she disliked being pulled through the close-set trees. She began to moo.

'Oh, don't do that!' said Jack, scared. 'You will give us away, Daisy.'

'Moo-oo-oo!' said Daisy sorrowfully, trying her hardest to stand still. But Jack and Mike pulled her on.

It was hard work getting her down to the boat. It took the boys at least two hours before they were by the lake, panting and hot. Daisy had mooed dozens of times, each time more loudly than before, and Jack was beginning to think that his idea of taking her across to the island was not such a good one after all. Suppose her mooing gave them away, and people came after them? Suppose she mooed a great deal on the island? Whatever would they do?

Still, they had at last got her to the boat. Jack persuaded the poor, frightened cow to step into the water. She gave such a moo that she startled even the two boys. But at last she was in the water. The boys got into the boat, and pushed off. Jack had tied the cow's rope to the stern of the boat. The boys bent to their oars, and poor Daisy found that she was being pulled off her feet into deeper water!

It was a dreadful adventure for a cow who had never been out of her field before, except to be milked in a nearby shed! She waggled her long legs about, and began to swim in a funny sort of way, holding her big head high out of the water. She was too frightened to moo.

Jack lighted the lantern and fixed it to the front of the boat. It was very dark and he wanted to see where he was going. Then off they rowed up the lake towards the secret island, and Daisy the cow came after them, not able to help herself.

'Well, my idea is working,' said Jack after a bit.

'Yes,' said Mike, 'but I'm jolly glad it's only one cow we're taking, not a whole herd!'

They said no more till they came in sight of the island, which loomed up near by, black and solid. The girls had heard the splashing of the oars, and had come down to the beach with the candle.

'Have you got the cow, Jack?' they called.

'Yes,' shouted back the boys. 'She's come along behind beautifully. But she doesn't like it, poor creature!'

They pulled the boat up the beach and then dragged out the shivering, frightened cow. Jack spoke to her kindly and she pressed against him in wonder and fear. He was the one thing she knew, and she wanted to be close to him. Jack told Mike to get a sack and help him to rub the cow down, for she was cold and wet.

'Where shall we put her for tonight?' asked Mike.

'In the hen-yard,' said Jack. 'She's used to hens and hens are used to her. There is a lot of bracken and heather there and we can put some more armfuls in for her to lie on. She will soon be warm and comfortable. She will like to hear the clucking of the hens, too.'

So Daisy was pushed into the hen-yard, and there she lay down on the warm heather, comforted by the sound of the disturbed hens.

The girls were so excited at seeing the cow. They asked the boys over and over again all about their adventure till Mike and Jack were tired of telling it.

'Jack! You do look awfully fat tonight!' said Nora suddenly, swinging the lantern so that its light fell on Jack. The others looked at him in surprise. Yes, he did look enormous!

'Have you swollen up, or something?' asked Peggy anxiously. Jack laughed loudly.

'No!' he said, 'I found some clothes of mine in a box and brought them along. As the easiest way to carry them was to wear them, I put them on. That's why I look so fat!'

It took him a long time to take all the clothes off, because they were all laughing so much. Peggy looked at the holes in them and was glad she had brought her work-basket along. She could mend them nicely! The blanket, too, would be useful on a cold night.

'What's that funny light in the sky over there?' said Nora, suddenly, pointing towards the east. 'Look!'

'You silly! It's the dawn coming,' said Jack. 'It must be nearly daylight! Come on, we really must go to sleep. What a night we've had!'

'Moo-oo-oo!' said Daisy, from the hen-yard, and the children laughed.

'Daisy thinks so, too!' cried Peggy.

CHAPTER EIGHT

A Lazy Day – with a Horrid Ending

THE NEXT morning the children slept very late indeed. The sun was high in the sky before anyone stirred, and even then they might not have awakened if Daisy the cow hadn't decided that it was more than time for her to be milked. She stood in the hen-yard and bellowed for all she was worth.

Jack sat up, his heart thumping loudly. Whatever was that awful noise? Of course – it was Daisy! She wanted to be milked!

'Hi, you others!' he shouted. 'Wake up! It must be about nine o'clock! Look at the sun, it's very high! And Daisy wants to be milked!'

Mike grunted and opened his eyes. He felt very sleepy after his late night. The girls sat up and rubbed their eyes. Daisy bellowed again, and the hens clucked in fright.

'Our farmyard wants its breakfast,' grinned Jack. 'Come on, lazybones, come and help. We'll have to see to them before we get our own meal.'

They scrambled up. They were so very sleepy that they

simply had to run down to the lake and dip their heads into the water before they could do anything!

Then they all went to gloat over their cow. How pretty she was in her brown and white coat! How soft and brown her eyes were! A cow of their own! How lovely!

'And what a voice she has!' said Jack, as the cow mooed again. 'I must milk her.'

'But I say – we haven't a pail!' said Mike.

The children stared at one another in dismay. It was true – they had no pail.

'Well, we must use the saucepans,' said Jack firmly. 'And we can all do with a cup or two of milk to start the day. I'll use the biggest saucepan, and when it's full I'll have to pour it into the bowls and jugs we've got – and the kettle, too. We must certainly get a pail. What a pity I didn't think of it last night!'

There was more than enough milk to fill every bowl and jug and saucepan. The children drank cupful after cupful. It was lovely to have milk after drinking nothing but tea and cocoa made with water. They could not have enough of it!

'I say! Daisy has trodden on a hen's egg and smashed it,' said Nora, looking into the hen-yard. 'What a pity!'

'Never mind,' said Jack. 'We won't keep her here after today. She shall go and live on that nice grassy piece, the other side of the island. Nora, feed the hens. They are clucking as if they'd never stop. They are hungry.'

Nora fed them. Then they all sat down to their breakfast of boiled eggs and creamy milk. Daisy the cow looked at them as they ate, and mooed softly. She was hungry, too.

Jack and Mike took her to the other side of the island after they had finished their meal. She was delighted to see the juicy green grass there and set to work at once, pulling mouthfuls of it as she wandered over the field.

'She can't get off the island, so we don't need to fence her in,' said Jack. 'We must milk her twice a day, Mike. We must certainly get a pail from somewhere.'

'There's an old milking-pail in the barn at Aunt Harriet's farm,' said Peggy. 'I've seen it hanging there often.'

'Has it got a hole in it?' asked Jack. 'If it has it's no use to us. We'll have to stand our milk in it all day and we don't want it to leak away.'

'No, it doesn't leak,' said Peggy. 'I filled it with water one day to take to the hens. It's only just a very old one and not used now.'

'I'll go and get it tonight,' said Mike.

'No, I'll go,' said Jack. 'You might be caught.'

'Well, so might you,' said Mike. 'We'll go together.'

'Can't we come, too?' asked the girls.

'Certainly not,' said Jack, at once. 'There's no use the whole lot of us running into danger.'

'How shall we keep the milk cool?' wondered Peggy. 'It's jolly hot on this island.'

'I'll make a little round place to fit the milk-pail into, just by one of the springs,' said Jack, at once. 'Then, with the cool spring water running round the milk-pail all day, the milk will keep beautifully fresh and cool.'

'How clever you are, Jack!' said Nora.

'No, I'm not,' said Jack. 'It's just common sense, that's all. Anyone can think of things like that.'

'I do feel tired and stiff today,' said Mike, stretching out his arms. 'It was pretty hard work pulling old Daisy along last night!'

'We'd better have a restful day,' said Jack, who was also feeling tired. 'For once in a while we won't do anything. We'll just lie about and read and talk.'

The children had a lovely day. They bathed three times, for it was very hot. Nora washed the two big roller towels in the lake, and made them clean. They soon dried in the hot sun, and then the two boys took one for themselves and the two girls had the other. How nice it was to dry themselves on towels instead of on rough sacks!

'Fish for dinner,' said Jack, going down to look at his lines.

A LAZY DAY – WITH A HORRID ENDING

'And custard!' said Nora, who had been doing some cooking with eggs and milk.

'Well, I feel just as hungry as if I'd been hard at work building all morning!' said Mike.

The afternoon passed by lazily. The boys slept. Nora read a book. Peggy got out her work-basket and began on the long, long task of mending up the old clothes Jack had brought back the night before. She thought they would be very useful indeed when the cold weather came. She wished she and Nora and Mike could get some of their clothes, too.

The hens clucked in the hen-yard. Daisy the cow mooed once or twice, feeling rather strange and lonely – but she seemed to be settling down very well.

'I hope she won't moo too much,' thought Peggy, her needle flying in and out busily. 'She might give us away with her mooing if anyone came up the lake in a boat. But thank goodness no one ever does!'

Everyone felt very fresh after their rest. They decided to have a walk round the island. Nora fed the hens and then they set off.

It was a nice little island. Trees grew thickly down to the waterside all round. The steep hill that rose in the middle was a warm, sunny place, covered with rabbit runs and burrows. The grassy piece beyond the hill was full of

73

little wild flowers, and birds sang in the bushes around. The children peeped into the dark caves that ran into the hillside, but did not feel like exploring them just then, for they had no candles with them.

'I'll take you to the place where wild raspberries grow,' said Jack. He led them round the hill to the west side, and there, in the blazing sun, the children saw scores of raspberry canes, tangled and thick.

'Jack! There are some getting ripe already!' cried Nora, in delight. She pointed to where spots of bright red dotted the canes. The children squeezed their way through and began to pick the raspberries. How sweet and juicy they were!

'We'll have some of these with cream each day,' said Peggy. 'I can skim the cream off the cow's milk, and we will have raspberries and cream for supper. Oooh!'

'Oooh!' said everyone, eating as fast as they could.

'Are there any wild strawberries on the island, too?' asked Nora.

'Yes,' said Jack, 'but they don't come till later. We'll look for those in August and September.'

'I do think this is a lovely island,' said Peggy happily. 'We've a splendid house of our own – hens, a cow, wild fruit growing, fresh water each day!'

'It's all right now it's warm weather,' said Jack. 'It won't

74

be quite so glorious when the cold winds begin to blow! But winter is a long way off yet.'

They climbed up the west side of the hill, which was very rocky. They came to a big rock right on the very top, and sat there. The rock was so warm that it almost burnt them. From far down below the blue spire of smoke rose up from the fire.

'Let's play a game,' said Jack. 'Let's play—'

But what game Jack wanted the others never knew – for Jack suddenly stopped, sat up very straight, and stared fixedly down the blue, sparkling lake. The others sat up and stared, too. And what they saw gave them a dreadful shock!

'Some people in a boat!' said Jack. 'Do you see them? Away down there!'

'Yes,' said Mike, going pale. 'Are they after us, do you think?'

'No,' said Jack, after a while. 'I think I can hear a radio playing – and if it was anyone after us they surely wouldn't bring that! They are probably just day-trippers, from the village at the other end of the lake.'

'Do you think they'll come to the island?' asked Peggy.

'I don't know,' said Jack. 'They may – but anyway it would only be for a little while. If we can hide all traces of our being here they won't know a thing about us.'

'Come on, then,' said Mike, slipping off the rock. 'We'd better hurry. It won't be long before they're here.'

The children hurried down to the beach. Jack and Mike stamped out the fire, and carried the charred wood to the bushes. They scattered clean sand over the place where they had the fire. They picked up all their belongings and hid them.

'I don't think anyone would find Willow House,' said Jack. 'The trees really are too thick all round it for any day-tripper to bother to squeeze through.'

'What about the hens?' said Peggy.

'We'll catch them and pop them into a sack just for now,' said Jack. 'The hen-yard will have to stay. I don't think anyone will find it – it's well hidden. But we certainly couldn't have the hens clucking away there!'

'And Daisy the cow?' said Peggy, looking worried.

'We'll watch and see which side of the island the day-trippers come,' said Jack. 'As far as I know, there is only one landing place, and that is our beach. As Daisy is right on the other side of the island, they are not likely to see her unless they go exploring. And let's hope they don't do that!'

'Where shall we hide?' said Nora.

'We'll keep a look-out from the hill, hidden in the bracken,' said Jack. 'If the day-trippers begin to wander about, we must just creep about in the bracken and trust to luck they won't see us. There's one thing – they won't be *looking* for us, if they are day-trippers. They won't guess there is anyone else here at all!'

'Will they find the things in the cave-larder?' asked Nora, helping to catch the squawking hens.

'Peggy, get some heather and bracken and stuff up the opening to the cave-larder,' said Jack. Peggy ran off at once. Jack put the hens gently into the sack one by one and ran up the hill with them. He went to the other side of the hill and came to one of the caves he knew. He called to Nora, who was just behind him.

'Nora! Sit at the little opening here and see that the hens don't get out! I'm going to empty them out of the sack into the cave!'

With much squawking and scuffling and clucking the scared hens hopped out of the sack and ran into the little cave. Nora sat down at the entrance, hidden by the bracken that grew there. No hen could get out whilst she was there.

'The boat is going round the island,' whispered Jack as he parted the bracken at the top of the hill and looked down to the lake below. 'They can't find a place to land. They're going round to our little beach! Well – Daisy the cow is safe, if they don't go exploring! Hope she doesn't moo!'

CHAPTER NINE

The Day-Trippers Come to the Island

NORA SAT crouched against the entrance of the little cave. She could hear the six hens inside, clucking softly as they scratched about. Jack knelt near her, peering through the bracken, trying to see what the boat was doing.

'Mike has rowed our own boat to where the brambles fall over the water, and has pushed it under them,' said Jack, in a low voice. 'I don't know where he is now. I can't see him.'

'Where's Peggy?' whispered Nora.

'Here I am,' said a low voice, and Peggy's head popped up above the bracken a little way down the hill. 'I say – isn't this horrid? I do wish those people would go away.'

The sound of voices came up the hillside from the lake below.

'Here's a fine landing place!' said one voice.

'They've found our beach,' whispered Jack.

'Pull the boat in,' said a woman's voice. 'We'll have our supper here. It's lovely!'

There was the sound of a boat being pulled a little

way up the beach. Then the day-trippers got out.

'I'll bring the radio,' said someone. 'You bring the supper things, Eddie.'

'Do you suppose anyone has ever been on this little island before?' said a man's voice.

'No!' said someone else. 'The countryside round about is quite deserted – no one ever comes here, I should think.'

The three children crouched down in the bracken and listened. The day-trippers were setting out their supper. One of the hens in the cave began to cluck loudly. Nora thought it must have laid an egg.

'Do you hear that noise?' said one of the day-trippers. 'Sounds like a hen to me!'

'Don't be silly, Eddie,' said a woman's voice scornfully. 'How could a hen be on an island like this! That must have been a blackbird or something.'

Jack giggled. It seemed very funny to him that a hen's cluck should be thought like a blackbird's clear song.

'Pass the salt,' said someone. 'Thanks. I say! Isn't this a fine little island! Sort of secret and mysterious. What about exploring it after supper?'

'That's a good idea,' said Eddie's voice. 'We will!'

The children looked at one another in dismay. Just the one thing they had hoped the day-trippers wouldn't do!

79

'Where's Mike, do you suppose?' said Peggy, in a low voice. 'Do you think he's hiding in our boat?'

'I expect so,' whispered Jack. 'Don't worry about him. He can look after himself all right.'

'Oh, my goodness! There's Daisy beginning to moo!' groaned Peggy, as a dismal moo reached her ears. 'She knows it is time she was milked.'

'And just wouldn't I like a cup of milk!' said Jack, who was feeling very thirsty.

'Can you hear that cow mooing somewhere?' said one of the day-trippers, in surprise.

'I expect it's a cow in a field on the mainland,' said another lazily. 'You don't suppose there is a cow wandering loose on this tiny island, do you, Eddie?'

'Well, I don't know,' said Eddie, in a puzzled voice. 'Look over there. Doesn't that look like a footprint in the sand to you?'

The children held their breath. Could it be true that they had left a footprint on the sand?

'And see here,' went on the day-tripper, holding up something. 'Here's a piece of string I found on the beach. String doesn't grow, you know.'

'You are making a great mystery about nothing,' said one of the women crossly. 'Other day-trippers have been here, that's all.'

THE DAY-TRIPPERS COME TO THE ISLAND

'Perhaps you are right,' said Eddie. 'But all the same, I'm going to explore the island after supper!'

'Oh, put on the radio, Eddie,' said someone. 'I'm tired of hearing you talk so much.'

Soon loud music blared through the air, and the children were glad, for they knew it would drown any sound of Daisy's mooing or the hens' clucking. They sat in the bracken, looking scared and miserable. They did not like anyone else sharing their secret island. And what would happen if the day-trippers did explore the island and found the children?

Nora began to cry softly. Tears ran down her cheeks and fell on her hands. Jack looked at her and then crept silently up. He slipped his arm round her.

'Don't cry, Nora,' he said. 'Perhaps they won't have time to explore. It is getting a bit dark now. Do you see that big black cloud coming up? It will make the night come quickly, and perhaps the day-trippers will think there's a storm coming and row off.'

Nora dried her eyes and looked up. There certainly was a big black cloud.

'It looks like a thunderstorm,' said Peggy, creeping up to join them.

'Oooh!' said Nora suddenly, almost squealing out loud. 'Look! Someone's coming up the hill! I can see the bracken moving! It must be one of the day-trippers creeping up to find us!'

The children went pale. They looked to where Nora pointed – and sure enough they could see first one frond of bracken moving, and then another and another. Someone was certainly creeping up the hill hidden under the fronds.

Nora clutched hold of Jack. 'Don't make a sound,' he whispered. 'No one can possibly know we're here. Keep quiet, Nora. We'll slip inside the cave if he comes much nearer.'

They sat silently watching the swaying of the tall bracken as the newcomer crept through it. It was a horrid moment. Was someone going to spring out on them?

'Get inside the cave, you two girls,' whispered Jack. 'I think you'll be safe there. I'm going to slip round the hill and come up behind this person, whoever he is.'

The girls crept just inside the cave and parted the bracken that grew around it to see what Jack was going to do. He was just slipping away when the person creeping up the hillside stopped his crawling. The bracken kept still. This was worse than seeing it move! Oh dear!

Then a head popped out of the bracken, and Nora gave a loud squeal.

'Mike!' she said. 'Mike!'

'Sh, you silly chump!' hissed Peggy, shaking her. 'You'll be heard by the day-trippers!'

Fortunately the radio was going loudly, so Nora's squeal was not heard. The three children stared in delight at Mike. It was he who had been creeping up through the bracken after all! What a relief! He grinned at them and put his head down again. Once more the bracken fronds began to move slightly as Mike made his way through them up to the cave.

'Oh, Mike,' said Nora, when he came up to them. 'You did give us such a fright. We thought you were a day-tripper coming after us!'

'I got a good view of them,' said Mike, sitting down beside the others. 'There are three men and two women. They are tucking into an enormous supper.'

'Do you think they'll explore the island as they said?' asked Peggy anxiously.

'Perhaps this thunderstorm will put them off,' said Mike, looking up at the black sky. 'My word, it's brought the bats out early! Look at them!'

Certainly the little black bats were out in their hundreds. The hot, thundery evening had brought out thousands of insects, and the bats were having a great feast, catching the flies and beetles that flew through the air.

It was the bats that sent the day-trippers away. One

of the women caught sight of two or three bats darting round under the trees, and she gave a shriek.

'Ooh! Bats! Ooh! I can't bear bats! I'm frightened of them. Let's pack up and go quickly!'

'I can't bear bats either!' squealed the other woman. 'Horrid little creatures!'

'They won't hurt you,' said a man's voice. 'Don't be silly.'

'I can't help it, I'm frightened of them,' said a woman. 'I'm going!'

'But I wanted to explore the island,' said Eddie.

'Well, you'll have to explore it another day,' said the woman. 'Just look at the sky, too – there's going to be a dreadful storm.'

'All right, all right,' said Eddie, in a sulky voice. 'We'll go. Fancy being frightened of a few bats!'

The children on the hillside stared at one another in delight. The day-trippers were really going. And no one had discovered them. Goody, goody!

'Good old bats!' whispered Jack. 'Would you think anyone would be scared of those little flitter-mice, Nora?'

'Aunt Harriet was,' said Nora. 'I don't know why. I think they are dear little creatures, with their funny black wings. Anyway, I shall always feel friendly towards them now. They have saved us from being found!'

Daisy the cow mooed loudly. Jack frowned. 'If only we

had milked Daisy before the day-trippers came!' he said.

'Did you hear that?' said one of the day-trippers. 'That was thunder in the distance!'

The four children giggled. Nora rolled over and stuffed her hands into her mouth to stop laughing loudly.

'Good old Daisy!' whispered Mike. 'She's pretending to be a thunderstorm now, to frighten them away!'

Nora gave a squeal of laughter, and Jack punched her. 'Be quiet,' he said. 'Do you want us to be discovered just when everything is going so nicely?'

The day-trippers were getting into their boat. They pushed off. The children heard the sound of oars, and peeped out. They could see the boat, far down below, being rowed out on to the lake. A big wind sprang up and ruffled the water. The boat rocked to and fro.

'Hurry!' cried a woman's voice. 'We shall get caught in the storm. Oh! Oh! There's one of those horrid bats again! I'll never come to this nasty island any more!'

'I jolly well hope you won't!' said Jack, pretending to wave goodbye.

The children watched the boat being rowed down the lake. The voices of the people came more and more faintly on the breeze. The last they heard was the radio being played once again. Then they saw and heard no more. The day-trippers were gone.

'Come on,' said Jack, standing up and stretching himself. 'We've had a very narrow escape – but thank goodness, no one saw us or our belongings.'

'Except that footprint and a bit of string,' said Mike.

'Yes,' said Jack, thoughtfully. 'I hope that man called Eddie doesn't read anywhere about four runaway children and think we might be here because of what he heard and found. We must be prepared for that, you know. We must make some plans to prevent being found if anyone comes again to look for us.'

A distant rumble of thunder was heard. Jack turned to the others. 'Not Daisy mooing this time!' he grinned. 'Come on, there's a storm coming. We've plenty to do. I'll go and get Daisy, to milk her. Nora and Mike, you catch the hens and take them back to the hen-yard – and Mike, make some sort of shelter for them with a couple of sacks over sticks, or something, so that they can hide there if they are frightened. Peggy, see if you can light the fire before the rain comes.'

'Ay, ay, Captain!' shouted the children joyfully, full of delight to think they had their island to themselves once more!

CHAPTER TEN

A Stormy Night in Willow House

THERE WAS certainly a thunderstorm coming. The sky was very black indeed, and it was getting dark. Nora and Mike caught the six hens in the little cave, bundled them gently into the sack, and raced off to the hen-yard with them. Mike stuck two or three willow sticks into the ground at one end of the hen-yard and draped the sack over them.

'There you are, henny-pennies!' said Nora. 'There is a nice little shelter for you!'

Plop! Plop! Plop! enormous drops of rain fell down and the hens gave a frightened squawk. They did not like the rain. They scuttled under the sack at once and lay there quietly, giving each other little pecks now and again.

'Well, that settles the hens,' said Mike. 'I wonder how Peggy is getting on with the fire.'

Peggy was not getting on at all well. The rain was now coming down fast, and she could not get the fire going. Jack arrived with Daisy the cow and shouted to Peggy:

'Never mind about the fire! Now that the rain's coming

down so fast you won't be able to light it. Get into Willow House, all of you, before you get too wet.'

'The girls can go,' said Mike, running to help Jack. 'I'll get the things to help you milk. My goodness – we haven't drunk all the milk yet that Daisy gave us this morning!'

'Put it into a dish and pop it in the hen-yard,' said Jack. 'Maybe the hens will like it!'

In the pouring rain Jack milked Daisy the cow. Soon all the saucepans and the kettle and bowls were full! Now, thought Jack, he simply *must* get that old milk pail that the girls had told him of at their Aunt's farm. It was such a tiring business milking a cow like this.

When the milking was finished, Jack took Daisy back to her grassy field on the other side of the island. Mike went to Willow House where the two girls were. It was dark there, and the sound of rain drip-drip-dripping from the trees all around sounded rather miserable.

Mike and the two girls sat in the front part of Willow House and waited for Jack. Mike was very wet, and he shivered.

'Poor old Jack will be wet through, too,' he said. 'Feel this milk, girls. It's as warm as can be. Let's drink some and it will warm us up. We can't boil any, for we haven't a fire.'

Jack came to Willow House dripping wet. But he was

grinning away as usual. Nothing ever seemed to upset Jack.

'Hello, hello!' he said. 'I'm as wet as a fish! Peggy, where did we put those clothes of mine that I brought to the island last night?'

'Oh yes!' cried Peggy, in delight. 'Of course! You and Mike can change into those.'

'Well, I don't know about that,' said Mike. 'Jack only brought three old vests, a shirt or two, and an overcoat.'

'Well, we can wear a vest each, and a shirt, and I'll wear the overcoat, and you can wrap the old blanket I brought all round you!' said Jack.

The boys took off their wet clothes and changed into the dry ones. 'I'll hang your wet ones out to dry as soon as the rain stops,' said Peggy, squeezing the rain out of them.

'I can't see a thing here,' said Mike, buttoning up his shirt all wrong.

'Well, light the lantern, silly,' said Jack. 'What do you suppose the candles are for? Nora, find the lantern and light it. It may want a new candle inside. You know where you put the candles, don't you? Over in that corner somewhere.'

Nora found the lantern. It did want a new candle inside. She found a box of matches and lighted the candle. Mike hung the lantern up on a nail he had put in the roof.

It swung there, giving a dim but cheerful light to the little party huddled inside Willow House.

'This really feels like a house now,' said Nora, pleased. 'I do like it. It's very cosy. Not a drop of rain is coming through our roof or the walls.'

'And not a scrap of wind!' said Jack. 'That shows how well we packed the walls with heather and bracken. Listen to the wind howling outside! We shouldn't like to be out in that! What a good thing we've got Willow House to live in! Our outdoor bedroom wouldn't be at all comfortable tonight!'

The thunderstorm broke overhead. The thunder crashed around as if someone were moving heavy furniture up in the sky.

'Hello! Someone's dropped a wardrobe, I should think!' said Jack, when an extra heavy crash came!

'And there goes a grand piano tumbling down the stairs!' said Mike, at another heavy rumble. Everyone laughed. Really, the thunderstorm *did* sound exactly like furniture being thrown about.

The lightning flashed brightly, lighting up the inside of Willow House. Nora was not sure that she liked it. She cuddled up to Mike. 'I feel a bit frightened,' she said.

'Don't be silly!' said Mike. 'You're as bad as those women day-trippers over the bats! There's nothing to be frightened of. A storm is a grand thing. We're perfectly safe here.'

'A storm is just a bit of weather being noisy!' laughed Jack. 'Cheer up, Nora. We're all right. You can think you're lucky you're not Daisy the cow. After all, we do know that a storm is only a storm, but she doesn't.'

Crash! Rumble! Crash! The thunder roared away, and the children made a joke of it, inventing all kinds of furniture rumbling about the sky, as each crash came. The lightning flashed, and each time Jack said. 'Thanks very much! The sky keeps striking matches, and the wind keeps blowing them out!'

Even Nora laughed, and soon she forgot to be frightened. The rain pelted down hard, and the only thing that worried Jack was whether or not a rivulet of rain might find its way into Willow House and run along the floor on which they were sitting. But all was well. No rain came in at all.

Gradually the storm died away, and only the pitter-patter of raindrops falling from the trees could be heard, a singing, liquid sound. The thunder went farther and farther away. The lightning flashed for the last time. The storm was over.

'Now we'll have something to eat and a cup of milk to drink, and off to bed we'll go,' said Jack. 'We've had quite enough excitement for today! And Mike and I were so late last night that I'm sure he's dropping asleep. I know I am.'

Peggy got a small meal for them all, and they drank Daisy's creamy milk. Then the girls went into the back room of Willow House and snuggled down on the warm heather there, and the boys lay down in the front room. In half a minute everyone was asleep!

Again Daisy the cow awoke them with her mooing. It was strange to wake up in Willow House instead of in their outdoor sleeping place among the gorse, with the sky above them. The children blinked up at their green roof, for leaves were growing from the willow branches that were interlaced for a ceiling. It was dim inside Willow House. The door was shut, and there were no windows. Jack had thought it would be too difficult to make windows, and they might let in the wind and the rain too much. So Willow House was rather dark and a bit stuffy when the door was shut – but nobody minded that! It really made it all the more exciting!

The children ran out of Willow House and looked around – all except Nora. She lay lazily on her back, looking up at the green ceiling, thinking how soft the heather was and how nice Willow House smelt. She was always the last out of bed!

A STORMY NIGHT IN WILLOW HOUSE

'Nora, you won't have time for a dip before breakfast if you don't come now,' shouted Peggy. So Nora ran out, too. What a lovely morning it was! The thunderstorm had cleared away and left the world looking clean and newly washed. Even the pure blue sky seemed washed, too.

The lake was as blue as the sky. The trees still dripped a little with the heavy rain of the night before, and the grass and heather were damp to the foot.

'The world looks quite new,' said Mike. 'Just as if it had been made this very morning! Come on – let's have our dip!'

Splash! Into the lake they went. Mike and Jack could both swim. Jack swam like a fish. Peggy could swim a little way, and Nora hardly at all. Jack was teaching her, but she was a bit of a baby and would not get her feet off the sandy bed of the lake.

Peggy was first out of the water and went to get the breakfast – but when she looked round their little beach, she stood still in disgust!

'Look here, boys!' she cried. 'Look, Nora! How those day-trippers have spoilt our beach!'

They all ran out of the cold water, and, rubbing themselves down with their two towels, they stared round at their little beach, which was always such a beautiful place, clean and shining with its silvery sand.

93

But now, what a difference! Orange-peel lay every-where. Banana skins, brown, slippery, and soaked with rain, lay where they had been thrown. A tin that had once had canned pears in, and two cardboard cartons that had been full of cream, rolled about on the sand, empty. A newspaper, pulled into many pieces by the wind, blew here and there. An empty cigarette packet joined the mess.

The children felt really angry. The little beach was theirs and they loved it. They had been careful to keep it clean, tidy, and lovely, and had always put everything away after a meal. Now some horrid day-trippers had come there just for one meal and had left it looking like a rubbish-heap!

'And they were grown-up people, too!' said Jack, in disgust. 'They ought to have known better. Why couldn't they take their rubbish away with them?'

'People that leave rubbish about in beautiful places like this are just rubbishy people themselves!' cried Peggy fiercely, almost in tears. 'Nice people never do it. I'd like to put those people into a big dustbin with all their horrid rubbish on top of them – and wouldn't I bang on the lid, too!'

The others laughed. It sounded so funny. But they were all angry about their beach being spoilt.

'I'll clear up the mess and burn it,' said Mike.

'Wait a minute!' said Jack. 'We might find some of the things useful.'

'What! Old banana skins and orange-peel!' cried Mike. 'You're not thinking of making a pudding or something of them, Jack!'

'No,' said Jack, with a grin. 'But if we keep the tin and a carton and the empty cigarette packet in our cave-cupboard, we might put them out on the beach if anyone else ever comes – and then, if they happen to find the remains of our fire, or a bit of string or anything like that – why, they won't think of looking for us – they'll just think day-trippers have been here!'

'Good idea, Jack!' cried everyone.

'You really are good at thinking out clever things,' said Peggy, busy getting the fire going. Its crackling sounded very cheerful, for they were all hungry. Peggy put some milk on to boil. She meant to make cocoa for them all to drink.

Mike picked up the cigarette packet, the tin, and one of the cardboard cartons. He washed the carton and the tin in the lake, and then went to put the three things away in their little cave-cupboard. They might certainly come in useful some day!

Nora brought in five eggs for breakfast. Peggy fried

them with two trout that Jack had caught on his useful lines. The smell was delicious!

'I say! Poor old Daisy *must* be milked!' said Jack, gobbling down his breakfast and drinking his hot cocoa.

Suddenly Nora gave a squeal and pointed behind him. Jack turned – and to his great astonishment he saw the cow walking towards him!

'You wouldn't go to milk her in time so she has come to you!' laughed Peggy. 'Good old Daisy! Fancy her knowing the way!'

CHAPTER ELEVEN

Nora Gets into Trouble

THERE SEEMED quite a lot of jobs always waiting to be done each day on the island. Daisy had to be milked. The hens had to be seen to. The fishing lines had to be baited and looked at two or three times a day. The fire had to be kept going. Meals had to be prepared and dishes washed up. Willow House had to be tidied up each day, for it was surprising how untidy it got when the four children were in it even for an hour.

'I'll milk Daisy each morning and Mike can milk her in the evenings,' said Jack, as they sat eating their breakfast that morning. 'Nora, you can look after the hens. It won't only be your job to feed them and give them water and collect the eggs, but you'll have to watch the fence round the hen-yard carefully to see that the hens don't peck out the heather we've stuffed into the fence to stop up the holes. We don't want to lose our hens!'

'What is Peggy going to do?' asked Nora.

'Peggy had better do the odd jobs,' said Jack. 'She can look after the fire, think of meals and tidy up. I'll see to my fishing lines. And every now and again one or other of us had better go to the top of the hill to see if any more day-trippers are coming. Our plans worked quite well last time – but we were lucky enough to spot the boat coming. If we hadn't seen it when we did, we would have been properly caught!'

'I'd better go and get the boat out from where I hid it under the overhanging bushes, hadn't I?' said Mike, finishing his cocoa.

'No,' said Jack. 'It would be a good thing to keep it always hidden there except when we need it. Now I'm off to milk Daisy!'

He went off, and the children heard the welcome sound of the creamy milk splashing into a saucepan, for they still had no milking-pail. Mike and Jack were determined to get one that night! It was so awkward to keep milking a cow into saucepans and kettles!

Peggy began to clear away and wash up the dishes. Nora wanted to help her, but Peggy said she had better go and feed the hens. So off she went, making the little clucking noise that the hens knew. They came rushing to her as she climbed over the fence of their little yard.

Nora scattered the seed for them, and they gobbled it up, scratching hard with their strong clawed feet to find any they had missed. Nora gave them some water, too.

Then she took a look round the fence to see that it was all right.

It seemed all right. The little girl didn't bother to look very hard, because she wanted to go off to the raspberry patch up on the hillside and see if there were any more wild raspberries ripe. If she had looked carefully, as she should have done, she would have noticed quite a big hole in the fence, where one of the hens had been pecking out the bracken and heather. But she didn't notice. She picked up a basket Peggy had made of thin twigs, and set off.

'Are you going to find raspberries, Nora?' called Peggy.

'Yes!' shouted Nora.

'Well, bring back as many as you can, and we'll have them for pudding at dinnertime with cream!' shouted Peggy. 'Don't eat them all yourself!'

'Come with me and help me!' cried Nora, not too pleased at the thought of having to pick raspberries for everyone.

'I've got to get some water from the spring,' called back Peggy, 'and I want to do some mending.'

So Nora went alone. She found a patch of raspberries she hadn't seen yesterday, and there were a great many ripe. The little girl ate dozens and then began to fill her basket with the sweet juicy fruit. She heard Jack taking Daisy the cow back to her grassy field on the other side

99

of the island. She heard Mike whistling as he cut some willow stakes down in the thicket, ready for use if they were wanted. Everyone was busy and happy.

Nora sat down in the sun and leaned against a warm rock that jutted out from the hillside. She felt very happy indeed. The lake was as blue as a forget-me-not down below her. Nora lazed there in the sun until she heard Mike calling:

'Nora! Nora! Wherever are you? You've been hours!'

'Coming!' cried Nora, and she made her way through the raspberry canes, round the side of the hill, through the heather and bracken, and down to the beach, where all the others were. Peggy had got the fire going well, and was cooking a rabbit that Jack had produced.

'Where are the raspberries?' asked Jack. 'Oh, you've got a basketful! Good! Go and skim the cream off the milk in that bowl over there, Nora. Put it into a jug and bring it back. There will be plenty for all of us.'

Soon they were eating their dinner. Peggy was certainly a good little cook. But nicest of all were the sweet juicy raspberries with thick yellow cream poured all over them! How the children did enjoy them!

'The hens are very quiet today,' said Jack, finishing up the last of his cream. 'I haven't heard a single cluck since we've been having dinner!'

'I suppose they're all right?' said Peggy.

'I'll go and have a look,' said Mike. He put down his plate and went to the hen-yard. He looked here – and he looked there – he lifted up the sack that was stretched over one corner of the yard for shelter – but no hens were there!

'Are they all right?' called Jack.

Mike turned in dismay. 'No!' he said. 'They're not here! They've gone!'

'Gone!' cried Jack, springing up in astonishment. 'They can't have gone! They must be there!'

'Well, they're not,' said Mike. 'They've completely vanished! Not even a cluck left!'

All the children ran to the hen-yard and gazed in amazement and fright at the empty space.

'Do you suppose someone has been here and taken them?' asked Peggy.

'No,' said Jack sternly, 'look here! This explains their disappearance!'

He pointed to a hole in the fence of the hen-yard. 'See that hole? They've all escaped through there – and now goodness knows where they are!'

'Well, I never heard them go,' said Peggy. 'I was the only one left here. They must have gone when I went to get water from the spring!'

'Then the hole must have been there when Nora fed the hens this morning,' said Jack. 'Nora, what do you mean by doing your job as badly as that? Didn't I tell you this morning that you were to look carefully round the fence each time the hens were fed to make sure it was safe? And now, the very first time, you let the hens escape! I'm ashamed of you!'

'Our precious hens!' said Peggy, in dismay.

'You might do your bit, Nora,' said Mike. 'It's too bad of you.'

Nora began to cry, but the others had no sympathy for her. It was too big a disappointment to lose their hens. They began to hunt round to see if by chance the hens were hidden anywhere near.

Nora cried more and more loudly, till Jack got really angry with her. 'Stop that silly baby noise!' he said. 'Can't you help to look for the hens, too?'

'You're not to talk to me like that!' wept Nora.

'I shall talk to you how I like,' said Jack. 'I'm the captain here, and you've got to do as you're told. If one of us is careless we all suffer, and I won't have that! Stop crying, I tell you, and help to look for the hens.'

Nora started to hunt, but she didn't stop crying. She felt so unhappy and ashamed and sad, and it was really dreadful to have all the others angry with her, and not speaking a word to her. Nora could hardly see to hunt for the hens.

'Well, they are nowhere about here!' said Jack, at last. 'We'd better spread out and see if we can find them on the island somewhere. They may have wandered right to the other side. We'll all separate and hunt in different places. Peggy, you go that way, and I'll go over to Daisy's part.'

The children separated and went different ways, calling to the hens loudly. Nora went where Jack had pointed. She called to the hens, too, but none came in answer. Wherever could they be?

What a hunt there was that afternoon for those vanished hens! It was really astonishing that not one could be found. Jack couldn't understand it! They were nowhere on the hill. They were not even in the little cave where Jack had hidden them the day before, because he looked. They were not among the raspberry canes. They were not in Daisy's field. They were not under the hedges. They were not anywhere at all, it seemed!

Nora grew more and more unhappy as the day passed. She felt that she really couldn't face the others if the hens were not found. She made a hidey-hole in the tall bracken and crouched there, watching the others returning to the camp for supper. They had had no tea and were hungry and thirsty. So was Nora – but nothing would make her go and join the others! No – she would rather stay where she was, all alone, than sit down with Mike, Jack and Peggy while they were still so cross and upset.

'Well, the hens are gone!' said Mike, as he joined Jack going down the hill to the beach.

'It's strange,' said Jack. 'They can't have flown off the island, surely!'

'It's dreadful, I think,' said Peggy, 'we did find their eggs so useful to eat.'

Nora sat alone in the bracken. She meant to sleep there for the night. She thought she would never, never be happy again.

The others sat down by the fire, whilst Peggy made some cocoa, and doled out a rice pudding she had made. They wondered where Nora was.

'She'll be along soon, I expect,' said Peggy.

They ate their meal in silence – and then – then oh, what a lovely sound came to their ears! Yes, it was 'cluck, cluck, cluck!' And walking sedately down to the beach came all six hens! The children stared and stared and stared!

'Where *have* you been, you scamps?' cried Jack. 'We've looked for you everywhere!'

'Cluckluck, cluckluck!' said the hens.

'You knew it was your mealtime, so you've come for it!'

said Jack. 'I say, you others! I wonder if we could let the hens go loose each day – oh no – we couldn't – they'd lay their eggs away and we'd never be able to find them!'

'I'll feed them,' said Peggy. She threw them some corn and they pecked it up eagerly. Then they let Mike and Jack lift them into their mended yard and they settled down happily, roosting on the perch made for them at one end.

'We'd better tell Nora,' said Jack. So they went up the hillside calling Nora. 'Nora! Nora! Where are you?'

But Nora didn't answer! She crouched lower in the bracken and hoped no one would find her. But Jack came upon her suddenly and shouted cheerfully. 'Oh, there you are! The hens have all come back, Nora! They knew it was their mealtime, you see! Come and have your supper. We kept some for you.'

Nora went with him to the beach. Peggy kissed her and said, 'Now don't worry any more. It's all right. We've got all the hens safely again.'

'Had I better see to the hens each day, do you think, instead of Nora?' Mike asked Jack. But Jack shook his head.

'No,' he said. 'That's Nora's job – and you'll see, she'll do it splendidly now, won't you, Nora?'

'Yes, I will, Jack,' said Nora, eating her rice pudding,

and feeling much happier. 'I do promise I will! I'm so sorry I was careless.'

'That's all right,' said the other three together – and it was all right, for they were all kind-hearted and fond of one another.

'But what *I'd* like to know,' said Peggy, as she and Nora washed the dirty things, 'is *where* did those hens manage to hide themselves so cleverly?'

The children soon knew – for when, in a little while, Mike went to fetch something from Willow House he saw three shining eggs in the heather there! He picked them up and ran back to the others.

'Those cunning hens walked into Willow House and hid there!' he cried, holding up the eggs.

'Well, well, well!' said Jack, in surprise. 'And to think how we hunted all over the island – and those rascally hens were nearby all the time!'

CHAPTER TWELVE

The Caves in the Hillside

THE DAYS slipped past, and the children grew used to their happy, carefree life on the island. Jack and Mike went off in the boat one night and fetched the old milking-pail from Aunt Harriet's farm, and a load of vegetables from the garden. The plums were ripening, too, and the boys brought back as many as would fill the milking-pail! How pleased the girls were to see them!

Now it was easy to milk Daisy, for they had a proper pail. Peggy cleaned it well before they used it, for it was dusty and dirty. When Jack or Mike had milked Daisy they stood the pail of milk in the middle of the little spring that gushed out from the hillside and ran down to the lake below. The icy-cold water kept the milk cool, and it did not turn sour, even on the hottest day.

Jack got out the packets of seeds he had brought from his grandfather's farm, and showed them to the others. 'Look,' he said, 'here are lettuce seeds, and radish seeds, and mustard and cress, and runner beans! It's late to plant the beans, but in the good soil on this island I daresay they will grow quickly and we shall be able to have a crop later in the year.'

'The mustard and cress and radish will grow very quickly!' said Peggy. 'What fun! The lettuces won't be very long, either, this hot weather, if we keep them well watered.'

'Where shall we plant them?' asked Mike.

'Well, we'd better plant them in little patches in different corners of the island,' said Jack. 'If we dig out a big patch and have a sort of vegetable garden, and anyone comes here to look for us, they will see our garden and know someone is here! But if we just plant out tiny patches, we can easily throw heather over them if we see anyone coming.'

'Jack's always full of good ideas,' said Nora. 'I'll help to dig and plant, Jack.'

'We'll all do it,' said Jack. So together they hunted for good places, and dug up the ground there, and planted their precious seeds. It was Peggy's job to water them each day and see that no weeds choked the seeds when they grew.

'We're getting on!' said Nora happily. 'Milk and cream each day, eggs each day, wild raspberries when we want them, and lettuces, mustard and cress, and radishes soon ready to be pulled!'

THE CAVES IN THE HILLSIDE

Jack planted the beans in the little bare places at the foot of a brambly hedge. He said they would be able to grow up the brambles, and probably wouldn't be noticed if anyone came. The bean seedlings were carefully watched and nursed until they were strong and tall, and had begun to twist themselves round any stem near. Then Peggy left them to themselves, only watering them when they needed it.

It was sometimes difficult to remember which day it was. Jack had kept a count as best he could, and sometimes on Sundays the children could hear a church bell ringing if the wind was in the right direction.

'We ought to try and keep Sunday a day of rest and peace,' said Mike. 'We can't go to church, but we could make the day a *good* sort of day, if you know what I mean.'

So they kept Sunday quietly, and the little island always seemed an extra peaceful day then. They hardly ever knew what the other days were – whether it was Tuesday or Thursday or Wednesday! But Jack always told them when it was Sunday, and it was the one day they really knew. Nora said it had a different feel, and certainly the island seemed to know it was Sunday, and was a dreamier, quieter place then.

One day Jack said they must explore the caves in the hillside.

'If anyone does come here to look for us, and it's quite likely,' he said, 'we must really have all our plans made as to what to do, and know exactly where to hide. People who are really looking for us won't just sit about on that beach as the day-trippers did, you know – they will hunt all over the island.'

'Well, let's go and explore the cave today,' said Mike. 'I'll get the lantern.'

So, with the lantern swinging in his hand, and a box of matches ready in his pocket to light it, Jack led the way to the caves. The children had found three openings into the hillside – one where the hens had been put, another larger one, and a third very tiny one through which they could hardly crawl.

'We'll go in through the biggest entrance,' said Jack. He lighted the lantern, and went into the dark cave. It seemed strange to leave the hot July sunshine. Nora shivered. She thought the caves were rather eerie. But she didn't say anything, only kept very close to Mike.

Jack swung the lantern round and lit up all the corners. It was a large cave – but not of much use for hiding in, for every corner could be easily seen. Big cobwebs hung here and there, and there was a musty smell of bats.

Mike went all round the walls, peeping and prying – and right at the very back of the cave he discovered a curious thing. The wall was split from about six feet downwards, and a big crack, about two feet across, yawned there. At first it seemed as if the crack simply showed rock behind it – but it didn't. There was a narrow, winding passage there, half hidden by a jutting-out piece of rock.

'Look here!' cried Mike, in excitement. 'Here's a passage right in the very rock of the hillside itself. Come on, Jack, bring your lantern here. I wonder if it goes very far back.'

Jack lifted up his lantern and the others saw the curious half-hidden passage, the entrance to which was by the crack in the wall. Jack went through the crack and walked a little way down the passage.

'Come on!' he cried. 'It's all right! The air smells fresh here, and the passage seems to lead to somewhere.'

The children crowded after him in excitement. What an adventure this was!

The passage wound here and there, and sometimes the children had to step over rocks and piles of fallen earth. Tree roots stretched over their heads now and again. The passage was sometimes very narrow, but quite passable. And at last it ended – and Jack found that it led to an even larger cave right in the very middle of the hill itself! He lifted his lantern and looked round. The air smelt fresh and sweet. Why was that?

'Look!' cried Nora, pointing upwards. 'I can see daylight!'

Sure enough, a long way up, a spot of bright daylight came through into the dark cave. Jack was puzzled. 'I think some rabbits must have burrowed into the hill, and come out unexpectedly into this cave,' he said. 'And their hole is where we can see that spot of daylight. Well – the fresh air comes in, anyhow!'

From the big cave a low passage led to another cave on the right. This passage was so low that the children had to crawl through it – and to their surprise they found that this second cave led out to the hillside itself, and was none other than the cave into which it was so hard to crawl because of the small entrance.

'Well, we are getting on,' said Jack. 'We have discovered that the big cave we knew leads by a passage to an even bigger one – and from that big one we can get into this smaller one, which has an opening on to the hillside – and that opening is too small for any grown-up to get into!'

'What about the cave we put the hens into?' asked Nora.

'That must be just a little separate cave by itself,' said Jack. 'We'll go and see.'

So they squeezed themselves out of the tiny entrance of the last cave, and went to the hen-cave. But this was quite ordinary – just a little low, rounded cave smelling strongly of bats.

They came out and sat on the hillside in the bright sunshine. It was lovely to sit there in the warmth after the cold, dark caves.

'Now listen,' said Jack thoughtfully. 'Those caves are going to be jolly useful to us this summer if anyone comes to get us. We could get Daisy into that big inner cave quite well, for one thing.'

'Oh, Jack! She'd never squeeze through that narrow, winding passage,' said Peggy.

'Oh yes, she would,' said Jack. 'She'd come with me all right – and what's more, Daisy is going to practise going in and out there, so that if the time comes when she has really got to hide for a few hours, she won't mind. It wouldn't be any good putting her into that cave, and then having her moo fit to lift off the top of the hill!'

Everyone laughed. Mike nodded his head. 'Quite right,' he said. 'Daisy will have to practise! I suppose the hens can go there quite well, too?'

'Easily,' said Jack. 'And so can we!'

'The only things we can't take into the cave are our boat and our house,' said Mike.

'The boat would never be found under those brambles by the water,' said Jack. 'And I doubt if anyone would ever find Willow House either, for we have built it in the very middle of that thicket, and it is all *we* can do to squeeze through to it! Grown-ups could never get through. Why, we shall soon have to climb a tree and drop down to Willow House if the bushes and trees round it grow any more thickly!'

'I almost wish someone *would* come!' said Peggy. 'It would be so exciting to hide away!'

'A bit *too* exciting!' said Jack. 'Remember, there's a lot to be done as soon as we see anyone coming!'

'Hadn't we better plan it all out now?' said Mike. 'Then we shall each know what to do.'

'Yes,' said Jack. 'Well, I'll manage Daisy the cow, and go straight off to fetch her. Mike, you manage the hens and get them into a sack, and take them straight up to the cave. Peggy, you stamp out the fire and scatter the hot sticks. Also you must put out the empty cigarette packet, the tin, and the cardboard carton that the day-trippers left, so that it will look as if day-trippers have been here, and nobody will think it's funny to find the remains of a fire, or any other odd thing.'

'And what shall I do?' asked Nora.

'You must go to the spring and take the pail of milk from there to the cave,' said Jack. 'Before you do that scatter heather over our patches of growing seeds. And

Peggy, you might make certain the cave-cupboard is hidden by a curtain of bracken or something.'

'Ay, ay, Captain!' said Peggy. 'Now we've all got our duties to do – but you've got the hardest, Jack! I wouldn't like to hide Daisy away down that narrow passage! What will you do if she gets stuck?'

'She won't get stuck,' said Jack. 'She's not as fat as all that! By the way, we'd better put a cup or two in the cave, and some heather, in case we have to hide up for a good many hours. We can drink milk then, and have somewhere soft to lie on.'

'We'd better keep a candle or two in the entrance,' said Peggy. 'I don't feel like sitting in the dark there.'

'I'll tell you what we'll do,' said Jack thoughtfully. 'We won't go in and out of that big inner cave by the narrow passage leading from the outer cave. We'll go in and out by that tiny cave we can hardly squeeze in by. It leads to the inner cave, as we found out. If we keep using the other cave and the passage to go in, we are sure to leave marks, and give ourselves away. I'll have to take Daisy that way, but that can't be helped.'

'Those caves will be cosy to live in in the wintertime,' said Peggy. 'We could live in the outer one, and store our things in the inner one. We should be quite protected from bad weather.'

'How lucky we are!' said Nora. 'A nice house made of trees for the summer – and a cosy cave-home for the winter!'

'Winter's a long way off yet,' said Jack. 'I say! – I'm hungry! What about frying some eggs, Peggy, and sending Mike to get some raspberries?'

'Come on!' shouted Peggy, and raced off down the hillside, glad to leave behind the dark, gloomy caves.

CHAPTER THIRTEEN

The Summer Goes By

NO ONE came to interfere with the children. They lived together on the island, playing, working, eating, drinking, bathing – doing just as they liked, and yet having to do certain duties in order to keep their farmyard going properly.

Sometimes Jack and Mike went off in the boat at night to get something they needed from either Jack's farm or Aunt Harriet's. Mike managed to get into his aunt's house one night and get some of his and the girls' clothes – two or three dresses for the girls, and a coat and shorts for himself. Clothes were rather a difficulty, for they got dirty and ragged on the island, and as the girls had none to change into, it was difficult to keep their dresses clean and mended.

Jack got a good deal of fruit and a regular amount of potatoes and turnips from his grandfather's farm, which still had not been sold. There was always enough to eat, for there were eggs, rabbits, and fish, and Daisy gave them more than enough milk to drink.

Their seeds grew quickly. It was a proud day when Peggy was able to cut the first batch of mustard and cress and the first lettuce and mix it up into a salad to eat with hard-boiled eggs! The radishes, too, tasted very good, and were so hot that even Jack's eyes watered when he ate them! Things grew amazingly well and quickly on the island.

The runner beans were now well up to the top of the bramble bushes, and Jack nipped the tips off, so that they would flower well below.

'We don't want to have to make a ladder to climb up and pick the beans,' he said. 'My word, there are going to be plenty – look at all the scarlet flowers!'

'They smell nice!' said Nora, sniffing them.

'The beans will taste nicer!' said Jack.

The weather was hot and fine, for it was a wonderful summer. The children all slept out of doors in their 'green bedroom', as they called it, tucked in the shelter of the big gorse bushes. They had to renew their beds of heather and bracken every week, for they became flattened with the weight of their bodies and were uncomfortable. But these jobs were very pleasant, and the children loved them.

'How brown we are!' said Mike one day, as they sat round the fire on the beach, eating radishes, and potatoes cooked in their jackets. They all looked at one another.

'We're as brown as berries,' said Nora.

'What berries?' said Mike. 'I don't know any brown berries. Most of them are red!'

'Well, we're as brown as oak apples!' said Nora. They certainly were. Legs, arms, faces, necks, knees – just as dark as could be! The children were fat, too, for although their food was an odd mixture, they had a great deal of creamy milk.

Although life was peaceful on the island, it had its excitements. Each week Jack solemnly led poor Daisy to the cave and made her squeeze through the narrow passage into the cave beyond. The first time she made a terrible fuss. She mooed and bellowed, she struggled and even kicked – but Jack was firm and kind and led her inside. There, in the inner cave, he gave her a juicy turnip, fresh-pulled from his grandfather's farm the night before. Daisy was pleased. She chewed it all up, and was quite good when she was led back through the passage once more.

The second time she made a fuss again, but did not kick, nor did she bellow quite so loudly. The third time she seemed quite pleased to go, because she knew by now that a fine turnip awaited her in the cave. The fourth time she even went into the cave by herself and made her way solemnly to the passage at the far end.

'It's an awfully tight squeeze,' said Mike, from the back. 'If Daisy grows any fatter she won't be able to get through, Jack.'

'We won't meet our troubles halfway,' said Jack cheerfully. 'The main thing is, Daisy likes going into the cave now, and won't make a fuss if ever the time comes when she has to be put there in a hurry.'

July passed into August. The weather was thundery and hot. Two or three thunderstorms came along, and the children slept in Willow House for a few nights. Jack suggested sleeping in the cave, but they all voted it would be too hot and stuffy. So they settled down in Willow House, and felt glad of the thick green roof above them, and the stout, heather-stuffed walls.

The wild raspberries ripened by the hundred. Wild strawberries began to appear in the shady parts of the island – not tiny ones, such as the children had often found round the farm, but big, sweet, juicy ones, even nicer than garden ones. They tasted most delicious with cream. The blackberries grew ripe on the bushes that rambled all over the place, and the children's mouths were always stained with them, for they picked them as they went about their various jobs.

Jack picked them on his way to milk Daisy, and so did Mike. Peggy picked them as she went to get water from the spring. Nora picked them as she went to feed the hens.

Nuts were ripening, too, but were not yet ready. Jack looked at the heavy clusters on the hazel trees and longed for them to be ripe. He went to have a look at the beans. They were ready to be picked! The runners grew up the brambles, and the long green pods were mixed up with the blackberry flowers and berries.

'Beans for dinner today!' shouted Jack. He went to fetch one of the many baskets that Peggy knew how to weave from willow twigs, and soon had it full of the juicy green beans.

Another time Jack remembered the mushrooms that used to grow in the field at the end of his grandfather's farm. He and Mike set off in the boat one early morning at the end of August to see if they could find some.

It was a heavenly morning. Mike wished they had brought the girls, too, but it would not do to take a crowd. Someone might see them. It was just sunrise. The sun rose up in the east and the whole sky was golden. A little yellowhammer sang loudly on a nearby hedge, 'Little bits of bread and no cheese!' A crowd of young sparrows chirruped madly in the trees. Dew was heavy on the grass, and the boys' bare feet were dripping wet. They were soaked to the knees, but they didn't mind. The early sun was warm, and all the world was blue and gold and green.

'Mushrooms!' said Jack, in delight, pointing to where two or three grew. 'Look – fresh new ones, only grown up last night. Come on! Fill the sack!'

There were scores in the field. Jack picked the smaller ones, for he knew the bigger ones did not taste so nice and might have maggots in them. In half an hour their sack was full and they slipped away through the sunny fields to where they had moored their boat.

'What a breakfast we'll have!' grinned Jack. And they did! Fried mushrooms and fried eggs, wild strawberries and cream! The girls had gone out strawberry hunting whilst the boys had gone to look for mushrooms.

Nora learnt to swim well. She and Peggy practised every day in the lake till Jack said they were as good as he and Mike were. They were soon like fish in the water, and tumbled and splashed about each day with yells and shrieks. Jack was clever at swimming under water and would disappear suddenly and come up just beside one of the others, clutching hard at their legs! What fun they had!

Then there came a spell of bad weather – just a few days. The island seemed very different then, with the sun gone, a soft rain-mist driving over it, soaking everything, and the lake water as cold as ice.

Nora didn't like it. She didn't like feeding the hens in

the rain. She asked Peggy to do it for her. But Jack heard her and was cross.

'You're not to be a fair-weather person,' he told her. 'It's all very well to go about happily when the sun is shining and do your jobs with a smile – but just you be the same when we get bad weather!'

'Ay, ay, Captain!' said Nora, who was learning not to be such a baby as she had been. And after that she went cheerfully out to feed the hens, even though the rain trickled down her neck and ran in a cold stream down her brown back.

They were rather bored when they had to keep indoors in Willow House when it rained. They had read all their books and papers by that time, and although it was fun to play games for a while, they couldn't do it all day long. Peggy didn't mind – she had always plenty of mending to do.

She showed the boys and Nora how to weave baskets. They needed a great many, for the baskets did not last very long, and there were always raspberries, strawberries, or blackberries to pick. Mike, Jack and Nora thought it was fun to weave all kinds and shapes of baskets, and soon they had a fine selection of them ready for sunny weather.

Then the sun came back again and the children lay about in it and basked in the hot rays to get themselves warm once more. The hens fluffed out their wet feathers and clucked happily. Daisy came out from under the tree which gave her shelter, and gave soft moos of pleasure. The world was full of colour again and the children shouted for joy.

The beans, radishes, lettuces, and mustard and cress grew enormously in the rain. Jack and Mike picked a good crop, and everyone said that never had anything tasted so delicious before as the rain-swollen lettuces, so crisp, juicy, and sweet.

All sorts of little things happened. The hole in the boat grew so big that one day, when Mike went to fetch the boat from its hiding place, it had disappeared! It had sunk into the water! Then Jack and Mike had to use all their brains and all their strength to get it up again and to mend it so that it would not leak quite so badly.

The corn for the hens came to an end, and Jack had to go and see if he could find some more. There was none at his grandfather's farm, so he went to Mike's farm – and there he found some in a shed, but was nearly bitten by a new dog that had been bought for the farm. The dog bit a hole in his trousers, and Peggy had to spend a whole morning mending them.

Another time there was a great alarm, because Nora said she had heard the splashing of oars. Jack rushed off to get Daisy, and Mike bundled the hens into a sack – but, as nothing more seemed to happen, Peggy ran to the top of the hill and looked down the lake.

No boat was in sight – only four big white swans, quarrelling among themselves, and splashing the water with their feet and wings!

'It's all right, boys!' she shouted. 'It's only the swans! It isn't a boat!'

So Daisy was left in peace and the hens were emptied out of the sack again. Nora was teased, and made up her mind that she would make quite certain it was a boat next time she gave the alarm!

One day Jack slipped down the hillside when he was reaching for raspberries and twisted his ankle. Mike had to help him back to the camp on the beach. Jack was very pale, for it was a bad twist.

Peggy ran to get some clean rags and soaked them in the cold spring water. She bound them tightly round Jack's foot and ankle.

'You mustn't use it for a while,' she said. 'You must keep quiet. Mike will do your jobs.'

So Jack had to lie about quietly for a day or two, and he found this very strange. But he was a sensible boy, and he knew that it was the quickest way to get better. Soon he found that he could hop about quite well with a stout hazel stick Mike cut for him from the hedges – and after a week or so his foot was quite all right.

Another time poor Peggy overbalanced and fell into a gorse bush below her on the hill. She was dreadfully scratched, but she didn't even cry. She went to the lake and washed her scratches and cuts, and then got the supper just as usual. Jack said he was very proud of her. 'Anybody else would have yelled the place down!' he said, looking at the scratches all over her arms and legs.

'It's nothing much,' said Peggy, boiling some milk. 'I'm lucky not to have broken my leg or something!'

So, with these little adventures, joys, and sorrows, the summer passed by. No one came to the island, and gradually the children forgot their fears of being found, and thought no more of it.

CHAPTER FOURTEEN

Jack Does Some Shopping

THE SUMMER passed away. The days grew gradually shorter. The children found that it was not always warm enough to sit by the campfire in the evenings, and they went to Willow House, where they could light the lantern and play games. Willow House was always cosy.

They had had to stuff the walls again with heather and bracken, for some of it crumbled away and then the wind blew in. All the willow stakes they had used in the making of the walls had put out roots, and now little tufts of green, pointed leaves jutted out here and there up the sticks! The children were pleased. It was fun to have walls and a roof that grew!

One day Mike got a shock. He went to get another candle for the lantern – and found that there was only one left! There were very few matches left, too, for although the children were careful with these, and only used one when the fire had gone out, they had to use them sometimes.

'I say, Jack, we've only got one candle left,' said Mike.

'We'll have to get some more, then,' said Jack.

'How?' asked Mike. 'They don't grow on trees!'

'Jack means he'll go and get some from somewhere,' said Peggy, who was mending a hole in Jack's shirt. She was so glad she had been sensible enough to bring her work-basket with her to the secret island. She could stop their clothes from falling to pieces by keeping an eye on them, and stitching them as soon as they were torn.

'But where could he get candles except in a shop?' said Mike.

'Well, I've been thinking,' said Jack seriously. 'I've been thinking very hard. The autumn is coming, when we shall need a better light in the evenings. We shall need another blanket, too. And there are all sorts of little things we want.'

'I badly want some more mending wool and some black cotton,' said Peggy. 'I had to mend your grey trousers with blue wool yesterday, Jack.'

'And I'll have to have some more corn for the hens soon,' said Nora.

'And it *would* be nice if we could get some flour,' said Peggy. 'Because if I had a bag of flour I could make you little rolls of bread sometimes – I just long for bread, don't you!'

'It would be nice,' said Jack. 'Well, listen, everyone. Don't you think it would be a good idea if I took the boat and went to the village at the other end of the lake and bought some of the things we badly need?'

The others all cried out in surprise.

'You'd be caught!'

'You haven't any money to buy things with!'

'Oh, don't go, Jack!'

'I shouldn't be caught,' said Jack. 'I'd be very careful. No one knows me at that village. Anyway, if you're afraid, I'll go on to the next village – only it's five miles away and I'd be jolly tired carrying back all the things we want.'

'But what about money, Jack?' said Peggy.

'I'd thought of that,' said Jack. 'If Mike will help me to pick a sackful of mushrooms early one morning, I could bring them back here, arrange them in the willow baskets we make, and then take them to the village to sell. With the money I get I'll buy the things we want.'

'Oh, that *is* a good idea, Jack,' said Peggy. 'If only you don't get caught!'

'Don't worry about that, silly,' said Jack. 'Now we'd better make out a list of things we want, and I'll try and get them when I go.'

'I wish we could have a book or two,' said Peggy.

'And a pencil would be nice,' said Nora. 'I like drawing things.'

'And a new kettle,' said Peggy. 'Ours leaks a bit now.'

'And a few more nails,' said Mike.

'And the flour and the wool and the black cotton,' said Peggy.

So they went on, making up a list of things they would like to have. Jack said them all over, and counted them up so that he wouldn't forget them.

'Mike and I will get the mushrooms from the field over the water tomorrow morning,' he said.

'And I say, Jack – do you suppose you could sell some wild strawberries if you took them?' asked Nora eagerly. 'I know where there are lots. I found a whole patch yesterday, ever so big, and very sweet!'

'That's a splendid idea,' said Jack, pleased. 'Look here, we'll make lots of little baskets today, and then we will arrange the mushrooms and strawberries neatly in them and I'll take them in the boat to sell. We should make a lot of money!'

The children were really excited. Mike went off to get a supply of thin willow twigs, and Peggy ran to get some rushes. She had discovered that she could make dainty baskets from the rushes, too, and she thought those would be nice for the strawberries.

Soon all four children were sitting on the sunny hillside among the heather, weaving the baskets. The boys were as good at it as the girls now, and by the time the sun was sinking there was a fine array of baskets. Peggy counted them. There were twenty-seven!

'I say! If we can fill and sell all those, Jack, you will have plenty of money to buy everything,' said Mike.

The children went to bed early, for they knew they would have to be up at dawn the next day. They had no watches or clocks, and the only way to wake up early was to go to bed early! They knew that. It was a warm night, so they slept in their outdoor bedroom among the gorse bushes, lying cosily on their heather beds. Nothing ever woke them now, as it had done at first. A hedgehog could crawl over Jack's legs and he wouldn't stir! A bat could flick Mike's face and he didn't even move.

Once a little spider had made a web from Peggy's nose to her shoulder, and when Nora awoke and saw it there she called the boys. How they laughed to see a web stretching from Peggy's nose, and a little spider in the middle of it! They woke Peggy up and told her – but she didn't mind a bit.

'Spiders are lucky!' she said. 'I shall have some luck today!' And so she did – for she found her scissors, which she had lost the week before!

The children awoke early, just as the daylight was putting a sheet of silver over the eastern sky. A robin was tick-tick-ticking near by and burst into a little creamy song when the children awoke. He was not a bit afraid of them, for they all loved the birds and fed them with crumbs after every meal. The robin was very tame and would often sit on Peggy's shoulder whilst she prepared the meals. She liked this very much.

They all got up and had their dip in the lake. Peggy thought of one more thing they wanted – a bar of soap! Their one piece was finished – and it was difficult to rub dirt off with sand, which they had to do now they had no soap. Jack added that to the list in his mind – that made twenty-one things wanted! What a lot!

'Mike and I won't be very long picking mushrooms,' he said, as he got into the boat and pushed off. 'You and Nora go and pick the strawberries, Peggy. Have a kettle boiling on the fire when we come back so that we can have something hot to drink. It's rather chilly this morning.'

How busy the four children were as the sun rose! Mike and Jack were away in the mushroom field, picking as many mushrooms as they could, and stuffing them into the big sack they carried. Nora and Peggy were picking the wild strawberries on the island. Certainly the patch Nora had found was a wonderful one. Deep red strawberries glowed everywhere among the pretty leaves, and some of the berries were as big as garden ones.

'Don't they look pretty in our little green baskets?' said

Peggy, pleased. The girls had taken some of their baskets with them, and had lined them with strawberry leaves first. Then neatly and gently they were putting the ripe strawberries in.

'I should think Jack could sell these baskets of strawberries for a pound each,' said Peggy. 'They are just right for eating.'

The girls filled twelve of the rush baskets, and then went back to light the campfire. It was soon burning well, and Peggy hung the kettle over the flames to boil. Nora went to feed the hens.

'I'll milk Daisy, I think,' said Peggy. 'It is getting about milking time, and the boys won't have time this morning. Watch the fire, Nora, and take the kettle off when it boils.'

Soon the boys were back, happy to show the girls such a fine collection of white mushrooms. Peggy had finished milking Daisy and there was soon hot tea for everyone. The tin of cocoa had long been finished, and was added to the list that Jack had in his mind.

Whilst the boys were having breakfast of fried eggs and mushrooms, with a few wild strawberries and cream to follow, the two girls were busy arranging the best mushrooms in the willow baskets, which were bigger and stronger than the rush strawberry ones. There were more than enough to fill the baskets.

Peggy and Nora carried the full baskets carefully to the boat. They put them safely at the far end and covered them with elder leaves so that the flies would not get at them. The flies did not like the smell of the elder leaves.

The boys set off in the boat. It had been arranged that they should both go to the far end of the lake, but that only Jack should go to sell their goods and to shop. One boy alone would not be so much noticed. Mike was to wait in the boat, hidden somewhere by the lakeside, till Jack returned. Mike had some cold cooked fish and some milk, for it might be some hours before Jack came back.

'Here's a good place to put the boat,' said Jack, as he and Mike rowed up the lake, and came in sight of the village at the far end. An alder tree leaned over the water by the lakeside, and Mike guided the boat there. It slid under the drooping tree and Jack jumped out.

'I can easily find my way to the village from here,' he said. 'I'll be as quick as I can, Mike.'

Jack had two long sticks, and on them he threaded the handles of the baskets of mushrooms and strawberries. In this way he could carry them easily, without spilling anything. Off he went with his goods through the wood, and Mike settled down in the boat to wait for his return.

Jack was not long in finding the road that led to the little village – and to his great delight he found that it was market-day there! A small market was held every Wednesday, and it happened to be Wednesday that day!

'Good!' thought Jack. 'I shall not be so much noticed if there is a crowd of people – and I should be able to sell my goods easily!'

The boy went to the little market place, calling 'Fine mushrooms! Ripe wild strawberries!' at the top of his voice.

When people saw the neat and pretty baskets of mushrooms and strawberries they stopped to look at them. Certainly they were excellent goods, and very soon Jack was selling them fast. Coins clinked into his pocket, and Jack felt very happy. What a nice lot of things he would be able to buy!

At last his sticks held no more baskets. The people praised him for his goods and the cleverly woven baskets, and told him to come again. Jack made up his mind that he would. It was a pleasant way of earning money, and he could buy all the things he needed if only he could get the money!

He went shopping. He bought a very large bag of flour. He bought wool and cotton for Peggy. He bought scores of candles and plenty of matches. He bought a new kettle and two enamel plates. Peggy was always wishing she had more dishes. He bought some storybooks, and two pencils and a rubber. A drawing-book was added to his collection, some nails, soap, butter for a treat, some bars of chocolate, some tins of cocoa, tea, rice – oh, Jack had a load to carry before he had done!

When he could carry no more, and his money was all gone, he staggered off to the boat. He kept thinking what fun everyone would have that night when he unpacked the bags and boxes!

Mike was waiting for him impatiently. He was delighted to see Jack, and helped him to dump the things into the boat. Then off they rowed, home to the secret island.

CHAPTER FIFTEEN

Jack Nearly Gets Caught

WHAT FUN it was that evening, unpacking all the things Jack had brought! Mike helped Jack to take everything to the beach, and Nora and Peggy jumped up and down and squealed with excitement.

'Flour! What a lot! I can make you rolls now to eat with your fish and eggs!' cried Peggy in delight. 'And here's my wool – and my cotton!'

'And two pencils for me – and a rubber – and a drawing-book!' cried Nora.

'And butter – oh, and *chocolate*!' yelled Mike. 'I've forgotten what chocolate tastes like!'

'Oh, Jack, you are clever,' said Peggy. 'Did you sell all the mushrooms and strawberries?'

'Every single basket,' said Jack. 'And what is more, the people told me to bring more next week – so I shall earn some more money, and lay in a good stock of things for the winter! What do you say to that?'

'Fine, Captain!' shouted everyone joyfully. 'We shall be as cosy as can be with candles to see by, nice things to eat, books to read, chocolate to nibble! Hurrah!'

'Have you brought the corn for my hens, Jack?' asked Nora anxiously.

'Yes, there it is!' said Jack. 'And what about this new kettle and enamel dishes, Peggy? I thought you'd like those.'

'Oh, Jack, isn't it all exciting?' cried Peggy. 'Look here – shall we have supper now – and look at all the things again afterwards – and then put them away carefully? You and Mike will have to put up shelves in Willow House for all these new stores!'

Talking all at once and at the tops of their voices the children set to work to get supper. This was a rabbit stew, with runner beans picked by Nora and a baked potato each, with raspberries and cream afterwards. And as a special treat Jack gave everyone half a bar of the precious chocolate! The children were so happy – they really felt that they couldn't be any happier! The girls had been lonely all day without the two boys, and it was lovely to be all together again.

After supper they cleared away and washed the dishes, and then stamped out the fire. They took everything to Willow House, and lighted the lantern that hung from the roof. Jack also lighted another candle to make enough light to see clearly all the treasures he had brought.

'I say! What a nice lot of matches!' said Mike. 'We'll have to store those carefully in a dry place.'

'And look at the books!' squealed Peggy. 'Jack can read them out loud to us in the evening. *Robinson Crusoe*, and *Stories from the Bible* and *Animals of the World* and *The Boy's Book of Aeroplanes*. What a lovely lot! It will be fun to read about Robinson Crusoe, because he was alone on the island, just as we are. I guess we could teach him a few things, though!'

Everyone laughed. 'He could teach us a few things, too!' said Jack.

Jack had really shopped very well. He had even bought a tin of treacle, so that sometimes, for a treat, Peggy could make toffee! He had got sugar, too, which would be nice in their tea and cocoa. Their own sugar had been finished long ago.

'And we needn't be too careful now of all our things,' said Jack, 'because I can go each week and sell mushrooms and strawberries and earn money to buy more.'

'But what will you do when the mushrooms and strawberries are over?' asked Peggy.

'Then there will be blackberries and nuts,' said Jack. 'They won't fetch so much money, but at any rate I can get enough to store up plenty of things for the winter. If we can get flour, potatoes, rice, cocoa, and things like that, we shall be quite all right. Daisy can always give us milk and cream, and we get lots of eggs from the hens, fish from the lake, and a rabbit or two. We are really very lucky.'

'Jack, read to us tonight,' begged Nora. 'It's so long since I heard a story.'

'We'll begin *Robinson Crusoe* first, then,' said Jack. 'That seems sort of suitable. By the way, Nora, can you read yourself?'

'Well, I wasn't very good at it,' said Nora.

'I think it would be a good idea if we all took a night each to read out loud,' said Jack. 'It's no good forgetting what we learnt. I'll read tonight – and you shall read tomorrow night, Nora.'

So, by the light of the two candles, Jack began reading the tale of Robinson Crusoe to the others. They lay on the heather, listening, happy to be together, enjoying the tale. When Jack shut up the book they sighed.

'That was lovely,' said Peggy. 'My goodness, Jack, I guess we could write an exciting book if we wrote down all our adventures on the island!'

'Nobody would believe them!' laughed Jack. 'Yet it's all true – here we are, living by ourselves, feeding ourselves, having a glorious time on a secret island that nobody knows!'

The next day Jack and Mike rigged up some shelves on

which to keep some of their new stores. It was fun arranging everything. The children soon began to make out their next list of things for Jack to buy when he went to market.

'We shall have to keep the days pretty carefully in future,' said Jack. 'I don't want to miss Wednesdays now because Wednesday is market day at the village. I shall get better prices then.'

So, the next Wednesday, once again there was a great stir just about dawn, and the four children hurried to their tasks of picking mushrooms and strawberries. They had made plenty of baskets again, and Jack and Mike set off two or three hours later with the boat, taking the full baskets with them.

For three or four weeks Jack went to market, sold all his goods, and bought a great many stores for the winter. He and Mike decided to store the bags and sacks of goods in the inner cave of the hillside, as there they would be quite dry – and, as the children would probably have to live in the caves in the winter, the stores would be quite handy there.

As the weeks went by there were not so many wild strawberries to be found. Mushrooms stopped growing in the field, and other market goods had to take their place. The children went nutting in the hazel trees and struck down great clusters of ripe nuts, lovely in their ragged green coats and brown shells. The girls picked baskets of big ripe blackberries, and Jack took these to the market instead of mushrooms and strawberries.

People soon grew to know him at the market. They wondered where he came from, but Jack never told them anything about himself.

'I just live by the lakeside,' he said, when people asked him where he lived. They thought he meant somewhere by the lake – they did not know he meant by the lakeside on the secret island – and certainly Jack was not going to tell them!

One day, for the first time, Jack saw a policeman in the village. This struck him as strange, for he had never seen one there before, and he knew that the village was too small to have a policeman of its own. It shared one with the village five miles away. Jack's heart sank – could the policeman have been told that a strange boy was about – and could he be wondering if the boy was one of the lost children! Jack began to edge away, though his baskets of nuts and blackberries were only half sold.

'Hi, you!' called the policeman suddenly. 'Where do you come from, boy?'

'From the lakeside, where I've been gathering blackberries and nuts to sell,' said Jack, not coming near the policeman.

'Is your name Mike?' said the policeman.

And then Jack knew for certain that the policeman had been told that maybe he, Jack, *was* one of the four runaway children – and he had come to find out.

'No, that's not my name,' said Jack, looking very innocent. 'Buy some nuts, Mister Policeman?'

'No,' said the policeman, getting a strip of paper out of his pocket, and looking at a photograph there. 'Come you here, my lad. I think you're one of the runaway children – let's have a look at you.'

Jack turned pale. If the policeman had a picture of him, he was caught! Quick as lightning the boy flung down the two sticks on which he had a dozen or so baskets strung, and darted off through the crowd that had gathered. Hands were put out to stop him, but he struggled away, tearing his jacket, but not caring for anything but to escape.

He slipped round a corner and into a garden. He darted round the cottage there and peered into the back garden. There was no one there – but there was a little henhouse at the side. Jack made up his mind quickly. He opened the door of the henhouse, slipped inside, and crouched down in the straw there, hardly daring to breathe. There were no hens there – they were scratching about in the little run outside.

Jack heard the sound of shouting and running feet, and he knew that people were looking for him. He crouched lower, hoping that no one had seen him dart into the cottage garden.

The running feet went by. The shouting died down. No one had seen him! Jack let out a big breath, and his heart thumped loudly. He was really frightened.

He stayed in the henhouse all day long. He did not dare to move out. He was hungry and thirsty and very cramped, but he knew quite well that if he slipped out he might be seen. He must stay there till night. He wondered what Mike would think. The girls would be anxious, too.

A hen came in, sat on a nesting-box and laid an egg. She cackled and went out again. Another came in and laid an egg. Jack hoped that no one would see him if they came looking for eggs that afternoon!

Someone did come for the eggs – but it was after tea and the henhouse was very dark. The door was opened and a head came round. A hand was stretched out and felt in all the boxes. The eggs were lifted out – the door was shut again! Jack hadn't been seen! He was crouching against the other side of the house, well away from the nesting-boxes!

The henhouse did not smell nice. Jack felt miserable as he sat there on the floor. He knew that by running away he had as good as told the policeman that he was one of the runaways. And now the whole countryside would be searched again, and the secret island would probably be explored, too.

'But if I hadn't run away the policeman would have caught me and made me tell where the others were,' thought the boy. 'If only I can get back to where Mike is waiting with the boat, and get back safely to the island, we can make preparations to hide everything.'

When it was dark, and the hens were roosting in the house beside him, Jack opened the door and slipped out. He stood listening. Not a sound was to be heard except the voices of people in the kitchen of the cottage near by.

He ran quietly down the path to the gate. He slipped out into the road – and then ran for his life to the road that led to the wood by the lakeside where Mike was waiting.

But would Mike be waiting there? Suppose people had begun to hunt already for the four children – and had found Mike and the boat! What then? How would he get back to the girls on the island?

Jack forgot his hunger and thirst as he padded along at top speed to where he had left Mike. No one saw him. It was a dark night, for the moon was not yet up. Jack made his way through the trees to the lakeside.

And then his heart leapt for joy! He heard Mike's voice! 'Is that you, Jack? What a time you've been! Whatever's happened?'

CHAPTER SIXTEEN

The Great Hunt Begins

JACK SCRAMBLED into the boat, panting. 'Push off, quickly, Mike!' he said. 'I was nearly caught today, and if anyone sees us we shall all be discovered!'

Mike pushed off, his heart sinking. He could not bear the idea of being caught and sent back to his uncle's farm. He waited till Jack had got back his breath and then asked him a few questions. Jack told him everything. Mike couldn't help smiling when he thought of poor Jack sitting with the hens in the hen-house – but he felt very frightened. Suppose Jack had been caught!

'This is the end of my marketing,' said Jack gloomily. 'I shan't dare to show my nose again in any village. They will all be on the look-out for me. Why can't people run away if they want to? We are not doing any harm – only living happily together on our secret island!'

After a bit Jack helped Mike to row, and they arrived at the island just as the moon was rising. The girls were on the beach by a big fire, waiting anxiously for them.

'Oh Jack, oh Mike!' cried Nora, hugging them both,

and almost crying with delight, at seeing them again. 'We thought you were never coming! We imagined all kinds of dreadful things! We felt sure you had been caught!'

'I jolly nearly *was*,' said Jack.

'Where is your shopping?' asked Peggy.

'Haven't got any,' said Jack. 'I had only sold a few baskets when a policeman spotted me. I've got the money for the ones I sold – but what's the good of money on this island, where you can't buy anything!'

Soon Jack had told the girls his story. He sat by the fire, warming himself, and drinking a cup of hot cocoa. He was dreadfully hungry, too, for he had had nothing to eat all day. He ate a whole rice pudding, two fishes, and a hard-boiled egg whilst he talked.

Everyone was very grave and solemn. They knew things were serious. Nora was really scared. She tried her hardest not to cry, but Jack heard her sniffing and put his arm round her. 'Don't be a baby,' he said. 'Things may not be so bad after all. We have all our plans laid. There is no real reason why anyone should find us if we are careful. We are all upset and tired. Let's go to bed and talk tomorrow.'

So to bed in Willow House they went. Jack took off his clothes and wrapped himself in the old rug because he said he smelt like hens. Peggy said she would wash his things the next day. They did not get to sleep for a long time because first one and then another of them would say something, or ask a question – and then the talking would all begin again.

'Now, nobody is to say another word!' said Jack at last, in his firmest voice.

'Ay, ay, Captain!' said everyone sleepily. And not another word was spoken.

In the morning the children awoke early, and remembered what had happened the day before. Nobody felt like singing or shouting or joking as they usually did. Peggy solemnly got the breakfast. Jack went off in his old overcoat to milk the cow, for his things were not yet washed. Mike got some water from the spring, and Nora fed the hens. It was not a very cheerful party that sat down to breakfast.

When the things were cleared away, and Peggy had washed Jack's clothes and set them out to dry, the children held a meeting.

'The first thing to do,' said Jack, 'is to arrange that someone shall always be on watch during the day, on the top of the hill. You can see all up the lake and down from there, and we should get good warning then if anyone were coming – we should have plenty of time to do everything.'

'Shall we have someone on guard during the night?' asked Nora.

'No,' said Jack. 'People are not likely to come at night. We can sleep in peace. I don't think anyone will come for a few days, anyhow, because I think they will search around the lakeside first, and will only think of the island later.'

'I think, as we are not going to the mainland for some time, we had better make a big hole in the boat and let her sink,' said Mike. 'I've always been afraid she might be found, although she is well hidden under the brambles. After all, Jack, if she is sunk, no one could possibly find her!'

'That's a good idea, Mike,' said Jack. 'We can't be too careful now. Sink her this morning. We can easily get her up again and mend her if we want her. Peggy, will you see that every single thing is cleared away that might show people we are here? Look, there's some snippings of wool, there – that sort of thing must be cleared up, for it tells a tale!'

'I'll see to it,' promised Peggy. Jack knew she would, for she was a most dependable girl.

'Every single thing must be taken to the caves today,' said Jack, 'except just those few things we need for cooking, like saucepan and kettle and so on. We can easily slip those away at the last minute. We will leave ourselves a candle or two in Willow House, because we can sleep there till we have to go to the caves.'

'Jack, what about the hen-yard?' asked Nora. 'It really does look like a yard now, because the hens have scratched about so much.'

'That's true,' said Jack. 'Well, as soon as we know we've got to hide, Mike can pull up the fence round the hen-yard and store it in Willow House. Then he can scatter sand over the yard and cover it with heather. It's a good thing you thought of that, Nora.'

'There's one thing, even if we have to hide away for days, we've enough food!' said Peggy.

'What about Daisy, though?' said Mike. 'She won't have anything to eat. A cow eats such a lot.'

'We should have to take her out to feed at night,' said Jack. 'And by the way, Peggy, don't light the fire for cooking until the very last minute and stamp it out as soon as you have finished. A spire of smoke gives us away more than anything!'

'What about someone hopping up to the hilltop now?' said Mike. 'The sun is getting high. We ought to keep a watch from now on.'

'Yes, we ought,' said Jack. 'You take first watch, Mike. I'll give you a call when it's time to come down. We'll take turns all day long. Keep watch all round. We don't know from which end of the lake a boat might come, though it's more likely to be from the end I was at yesterday.'

Mike sped up the hill and sat down there. The lake lay blue below him. Not a swan, not a moorhen disturbed its surface. Certainly no boat was in sight. Mike settled down to watch carefully.

The others were busy. Everything was taken up to the caves in the hillside and stored there. Nora left a sack by the hen-yard ready to bundle the hens into when the time came. She also put a pile of sand by the yard, ready for Mike to scatter after the fences had been pulled up. Nora was no longer the careless little girl she had been. Nor was she lazy any more. She had learned that when she did badly everyone suffered, so now she did her best – and it was a very good best too.

After a while Jack went up to take Mike's place on the hilltop. Mike set to work to sink the boat. She soon sank to the bottom of the water, under the bramble bushes. Mike felt sure that no one would ever know she was there.

Peggy went hunting round looking for anything that might give them away. She did not find very much, for all the children tidied up after any meal or game. Broken eggshells were always buried, uneaten food was given to the hens, and it was only things like snippings of wool or cotton that the wind had blown away that could be found.

Peggy went on guard next and then Nora. It was dull work, sitting up on the hilltop doing nothing but watch, so Nora took her pencil and drawing-book and drew what she could see. That made the time go quickly. Peggy took her mending. She always had plenty of that to do, for every day somebody tore their clothes on brambles. After every stitch Peggy looked up and down the lake, but nothing could be seen.

That evening Mike was on guard, and he was just about to come down to get his supper when he saw something in the distance. He looked carefully. Could it be a boat? He called Jack.

'Jack! Come quickly! I can see something. Is it a boat, do you think?'

Everyone tore up the hill and Jack looked hard. 'Well, if it's a boat, it's very small,' he said.

'It's something black,' said Nora. 'Whatever is it? Oh, I do hope it isn't anyone coming now.'

The children watched, straining their eyes. And suddenly the thing they thought might be a small boat flew up into the air!

'It's that black swan we saw the other day!' said Jack, with a squeal of laughter. 'What a fright it gave us! Look, there it goes! Isn't it a beauty?'

The children watched the lovely black swan flying

slowly towards them, its wings making a curious whining noise as it came. Nora went rather red, for she remembered how frightened she had been the first time she had heard a swan flying over the island – but nobody teased her about it. They were all too thankful it was only a swan, not a boat.

'There's no need to keep watch any more tonight,' said Jack, and they all went down the hill. Evening was almost on them. They sat by their fire and ate their supper, feeling happier than the day before. Perhaps after all no one would come to look for them – and anyway, they had done all they could now to get things ready in case anyone *did* come.

The next day the children kept watch in turn again, and the next. The third day, when Nora was on guard, she thought she saw people on the far side of the lake, where a thick wood grew. She whistled softly to Jack, and he came up and watched, too.

'Yes, you're right, Nora,' he said at last. 'There *are* people there – and they are certainly hunting for something or someone!'

They watched for a while and then they called the others. There was no fire going, for Peggy had stamped it out. They all crowded on to the hilltop, their heads peeping out of the tall bracken that grew there.

'See over there!' said Jack. 'The hunt is on! It will only be a day or two before they come over here. We must watch very carefully indeed!'

'Well, everything is ready,' said Peggy. 'I wish they would come soon, if they are coming – I hate all this waiting about. It gives me a cold feeling in my tummy.'

'So it does in mine,' said Mike. 'I'd like a hot-water bottle to carry about with me!'

That made everyone laugh. They watched for a while longer and then went down, leaving Jack on guard.

For two days nothing happened, though the children thought they could see people on the other side of the lake, beating about in the bushes and hunting. Mike went on guard in the morning and kept a keen watch. Nora fed the hens as usual and Jack milked Daisy.

And then Mike saw something! He stood up and looked – it was something at the far end of the lake, where Jack had gone marketing. It was a boat! No mistaking it this time – a boat it was, and a big one, too!

Mike called the others and they scrambled up. 'Yes,' said Jack at once. 'That's a boat all right – with about four people in, too. Come on, there's no time to be lost. There's only one place a boat can come to here – and that's our island. To your jobs, everyone, and don't be frightened!'

The children hurried off. Jack went to get Daisy. Mike

went to see to the hens and the hen-yard. Peggy scattered the dead remains of the fire, and caught up the kettle and the saucepan and any odds and ends of food on the beach to take to the cave. Nora ran to cover up their patches of growing seeds with bits of heather. Would they have time to do everything? Would they be well hidden before the boatload of people came to land on their secret island?

CHAPTER SEVENTEEN

The Island Is Searched

NOW THAT people had really come at last to search the island the children were glad to carry out their plans, for the days of waiting had been very upsetting. They had laid their plans so well that everything went smoothly. Daisy, the cow, did not seem a bit surprised to have Jack leading her to the inner cave again, and went like a lamb, without a single moo!

Jack got her safely through the narrow passage to the inner cave and left her there munching a turnip whilst he went to see if he could help the others. Before he left the outer cave he carefully rubbed away any traces of Daisy's hoofmarks. He arranged the bracken carelessly over the entrance so that it did not seem as if anyone went in and out of it.

Mike arrived with the hens just then, and Jack gave him a hand. Mike squeezed himself into the little tiny cave that led by the low passage to the inner cave, for it had been arranged that only Jack and the cow should use the other entrance for fear that much use of it should show too plainly that people went in and out.

Jack passed him the sack of hens, and Mike crawled on hands and knees through the low passage and into the big inner cave where Daisy was. The hens did not like being pulled through the tiny passage and squawked dismally. But when Mike shook them out of the sack, and scattered grain for them to eat, they were quite happy again. Jack had lighted the lantern in the inner cave, and it cast its dim light down. Mike thought he had better stay in the cave, in case the hens found their way out again.

So he sat down, his heart thumping, and waited for the others. One by one they came, carrying odds and ends. Each child had done his or her job, and with scarlet cheeks and beating hearts they sat down together in the cave and looked at one another.

'They're not at the island yet,' said Jack. 'I took a look just now. They've got another quarter-mile to go. Now, is there anything we can possibly have forgotten?'

The children thought hard. The boat was sunk. The cow and the hens were in. The fire was out and well scattered. The hen-yard was covered with sand and heather. The yard-fence was taken up and stored in Willow House. The seed patches were hidden. The milk pail was taken from the spring.

'We've done *every*thing!' said Peggy.

And then Mike jumped up in a fright. 'My hat!' he said. 'Where is it? I haven't got it on! I must have left it somewhere!'

The others stared at him in dismay. His hat was certainly not on his head nor was it anywhere in the cave.

'You had it on this morning,' said Peggy. 'I remember seeing it, and thinking it was getting very dirty and floppy. Oh, Mike! Where can you have left it? Think hard, for it is very important.'

'It might be the one thing that gives us away,' said Jack.

'There's just time to go and look for it,' said Mike. 'I'll go and see if I can find it.'

He crawled through the narrow passage and out into the cave with the low entrance. He squeezed through that and went out into the sunlight. He could see the boat from where he was, being rowed through the water some distance away. He ran down the hill to the beach. He hunted there. He hunted round about the hen-yard. He hunted by the spring. He hunted everywhere! But he could *not* find that hat!

And then he wondered if it was anywhere near Willow House, for he had gone there that morning to store the hen-yard fences. He squeezed through the thickly growing trees and went to Willow House. There, beside the doorway, was his hat! The boy pushed it into his pocket, and made his way back up the hillside. Just as he got to the cave entrance he heard the boat grinding on the beach below. The searchers had arrived.

He crawled into the big inner cave. The others greeted him excitedly.

'Did you find it, Mike?'

'Yes, thank goodness,' said Mike, taking his hat out of his pocket. 'It was just by Willow House – but I don't expect it would have been seen there, because Willow House is too well hidden among those thick trees to be found. Still, I'm glad I found it – I'd have been worried all the time if I hadn't. The boat is on the beach now, Jack; I heard it being pulled in. There are four men in it.'

'I'm just a bit worried about the passage to this inner cave from the outer cave,' said Jack. 'If that is found it's all up with us. I was wondering if we could find a few rocks and stones and pile them up halfway through the passage, so that if anyone *does* come through there, he will find his way blocked and won't guess there is another cave behind, where *we* are hiding!'

'That's a fine idea, Jack,' said Mike. 'It doesn't matter about the other entrance, because no grown-up could possibly squeeze through there. Come on, everyone. Find rocks and stones and hard clods of earth and stop up the passage halfway through!'

The children worked hard, and before half an hour had gone by the passage was completely blocked up. No one could possibly guess there was a way through. It would be quite easy to unblock when the time came to go out.

'I'm going to crawl through to the cave with the small entrance and peep out to see if I can hear anything,' said Jack. So he crawled through and sat just inside the tiny, low-down entrance, trying to hear.

The men were certainly searching the island! Jack could hear their shouts easily.

'*Some*one's been here!' shouted one man. 'Look where they've made a fire.'

'Day-trippers, probably!' called back another man. 'There's an empty tin here, too – and a carton – just the sort of thing day-trippers leave about.'

'Hi! Look at this spring here!' called another voice. 'Looks to me as if people have been tramping about here.'

Jack groaned. Surely there were not many footmarks there!

'Well, if those children are here we'll find them all right!' said a fourth voice. 'It beats me how they could manage to live here, though, all alone, with no food, except what that boy could buy in the village!'

'I'm going over to the other side to look there,' yelled the first man. 'Come with me, Tom. You go one side of the hill and I'll go the other – and then, if the little beggars are dodging about to keep away from us, one of us will find them!'

Jack felt glad he was safely inside the cave. He stayed where he was till a whisper reached him from behind.

'Jack! We can hear voices. Is everything all right?'

'So far, Mike,' said Jack. 'They are all hunting hard – but the only thing they seem to have found is a few footmarks round the spring. I'll stay here for a bit and see what I can hear.'

The hunt went on. Nothing seemed to be found. The children had cleared everything up very well indeed.

But, as Jack sat just inside the cave, there came a shout from someone near the beach.

'Just look here! What do you make of this?'

Jack wondered whatever the man had found. He soon knew. The man had kicked aside the heather that had hidden the hen-yard – and had found the newly scattered sand!

'This looks as if something had been going on here,' said the man. 'But goodness knows what! You know, I think those children *are* here somewhere. It's up to us to find them. Clever little things, too, they must be, hiding away all traces of themselves like this!'

'We'd better beat through the bushes and the bracken,'

said another man. 'They may be hiding there. That'd be the likeliest place.'

Then Jack heard the men beating through the bracken, poking into every bush, trying their hardest to find a hidden child. But not one could they find.

Jack crawled back to the cave after two or three hours and told the others what had happened. They listened, alarmed to hear that the hen-yard had been discovered even though they had tried so hard to hide it.

'It's time we had something to eat,' said Peggy. 'We can't light a fire in here, for we would be smoked out, but there are some rolls of bread I made yesterday, some wild strawberries, and a cold pudding. And lots of milk, of course.'

They sat and ate, though none of them felt hungry. Daisy lay down behind them, perfectly good. The hens clucked, quietly, puzzled at finding themselves in such a strange dark place, but quite happy with the children there.

When the meal was over Jack went back to his post again. He sat just inside the cave entrance and listened.

The men were getting puzzled and disheartened. They were sitting at the foot of the hill, eating sandwiches and drinking beer. Jack could hear their voices quite plainly.

'Well, those children *may* have been on this island, and

I think they were – but they're not here now,' said one man. 'I'm certain of that.'

'We've hunted every inch,' said another man. 'I think you're right, Tom; those kids have been here all right – who else could have planted those runner beans we found? – but they've gone. I expect that boy the policeman saw last Wednesday gave the alarm, and they've gone off in the boat.'

'Ah yes, the boat!' said a third man. 'Now, if the children were here we'd find a boat, wouldn't we? Well, we haven't found one – so they can't be here!'

'Quite right,' said the first man. 'I didn't think of that. If there's no boat here, there are no children! What about going back now? I'm sure it's no good hunting any more.'

'There's just one place we haven't looked,' said the quiet voice of the fourth man. 'There are some caves in this hillside – it's possible those children may have hidden there.'

'Caves!' said another man. 'Yes – just the place. We'll certainly look there. Where are they?'

'I'll show you in a minute,' said the fourth man. 'Got a torch?'

'No, but I've got plenty of matches,' said the other man. 'But look here – they can't be there if there's no boat anywhere to be seen. If they are here, there must be a boat somewhere!'

'It's possible for a boat to be sunk so that no searcher could find it,' said the fourth man.

'Children would never think of that!' said another.

'No, I don't think they would,' was the answer.

Jack, who could hear everything, thought gratefully of Mike. It had been Mike's idea to sink the boat. If he hadn't sunk it, it would certainly have been found, for the search had been much more thorough than Jack had guessed. Fancy the men noticing the runner beans!

'Come on,' said a man. 'We'll go to those caves now. But it's a waste of time. I don't think the children are within miles! They've gone off up the lakeside somewhere in their boat!'

Jack crawled silently back to the inner cave, his heart thumping loudly.

'They don't think we're on the island,' he whispered, 'because they haven't found the boat. But they're coming to explore the caves. Put out the lantern, Mike. Now everyone must keep as quiet as a mouse. Is Daisy lying down? Good! The hens are quiet enough, too. They seem to think it's night, and are roosting in a row! Now nobody must sneeze or cough – everything depends on the next hour or two!'

Not a sound was to be heard in the big inner cave. Daisy lay like a log, breathing quietly. The hens roosted peacefully. The children sat like mice.

THE ISLAND IS SEARCHED

And then they heard the men coming into the cave outside. Matches were struck – and the passage that led to their cave was found!

'Look here, Tom,' said a voice. 'Here's what looks like a passage – shall we see where it goes?'

'We'd better, I suppose,' said a voice. And then there came the sound of footsteps down the blocked-up passage!

CHAPTER EIGHTEEN

The End of the Search

THE CHILDREN sat in the inner cave as though they were turned into stone. They did not even blink their eyes. It seemed almost as if they did not even breathe! But how their hearts thumped! Jack thought that everyone must hear his heart beating, even the searchers outside, it bumped against his ribs so hard.

The children could hear the sound of someone fumbling his way along the narrow passage. He found it a tight squeeze, by his groanings and grumblings. He came right up to the place where the children had piled rocks, stones, and earth to block up the passage.

'I say!' the man called back to the others, 'the passage ends here in what looks like loose rocks. Shall I try to force my way through – pull the rocks to see if they are just a fall from the roof?'

'No!' cried another man. 'If you can't get through, the children couldn't! This is a wild-goose chase – we'll never find the children in these caves. Come back, Tom.'

The man turned himself round with difficulty and

began to squeeze back – and at the very moment a dreadful thing happened!

Daisy the cow let out a terrific moo!

The children were not expecting it, and they almost jumped out of their skins with fright. Then they clutched at one another, expecting the men to come chasing along at once, having heard Daisy.

There was an astonished silence. Then one of the men said, 'Did you hear that?'

'Of course!' said another. 'What in the wide world was it?'

'Well, it wasn't the children, that's certain!' said the first, with a laugh. 'I never in my life heard a child make a noise like *that*!'

'It sounded like a cow,' said another voice.

'A cow!' cried the first man, 'what next? Do you mean to say you think there's a cow in the middle of this hill, Tom?'

'Of course there can't be,' said Tom, laughing. 'But it sounded mighty like one! Let's listen and see if we hear anything again.'

There was a silence, as if the men were listening – and at that moment Daisy most obligingly gave a dreadful hollow cough, that echoed mournfully round and round the cave.

'I don't like it,' said a man's voice. 'It sounds too weird

for anything. Let's get out of these dark caves into the sunshine. I'm perfectly certain, since we heard those noises, that no children would be inside those caves! Why, they'd be frightened out of their lives!'

Jack squeezed Nora's hand in delight. So old Daisy had frightened the men! What a glorious joke! The children sat as still as could be, glad now that Daisy had given such a loud moo and such a dreadful cough.

There was the sound of scrambling about in the outer cave and then it seemed as if the men were all outside again. 'We'd better just hunt about and see if there are any more caves,' said one man. 'Look, that seems like one!'

'That's the cave where we put the hens when the day-trippers came!' whispered Jack. 'It's got no passage leading to our inner cave here. They can explore that all they like.'

The men did explore it, but as it was just a cave and nothing else, and had no passage leading out of it, they soon left it. Then they found the cave with the low-down, tiny entrance – the one the children used to squeeze into when they wanted to go to their inner cave – but, as Jack had said, the entrance was too small for any grown up to use, and, after trying once or twice, the men gave it up.

'No one could get in there except a rabbit,' said a man's voice.

THE END OF THE SEARCH

'Children could,' said another.

'Now look here, Tom, if we find children on this island now, I'll eat my hat!' said the first man. 'There's no boat, to begin with – and we really haven't found anything except runner beans, which might have been dropped by birds, and a funny sort of sandy yard – and you can't tell me children are clever enough to live here day after day, and yet vanish completely, leaving no trace behind, as soon as we come! No, no – no children are as clever as that!'

'I think you're right,' said Tom. 'Come on, let's go. I'm tired of this island with its strange noises. The sooner we get back home, the better I'll be pleased. Where those children have gone just beats me. I wish we could find them. There's such a surprise waiting for them!'

The voices grew distant as the men went down the hill to the beach, where they had put their boat. Jack crept quietly through the low passage into the small cave with the tiny entrance. He put his ear down to the entrance and listened. The sound of voices floated up to him. He heard the sound of oars being put ready. He heard the sound of the boat being pushed on to the water. Then came the sound of splashing.

'They're going!' he called. 'They really are!'

The others crowded round Jack. Then, when he thought it was safe, they all squeezed out of the tiny cave entrance and crept out on the hillside. Well hidden in the tall bracken, they watched the boatful of men being rowed away – away – away! The splashing of the oars, and the men's voices, came clearly to the four children as they stood there.

Nora suddenly began to cry. The excitement had been so great, and she had been so brave, that now she felt as if she must cry and cry and cry. And then Peggy began – and even Mike and Jack felt their eyes getting wet! This was dreadful – but oh, it was such a glorious feeling to know they had not been discovered, and that their dear little island, their secret island, was their very own again.

A low and mournful noise came from the inside of the hill – it was poor old Daisy the cow, sad at being left alone in the cave.

The children couldn't help laughing now! 'Do you remember how Daisy frightened those men!' chuckled Jack.

'She frightened me too,' said Peggy. 'Honestly, I nearly jumped out of my skin – if my dress hadn't been well buttoned up I believe I would have jumped *right* out of myself!'

That made the others laugh still more – and half-laughing, half-crying, they sat down on the hillside to wait till the boat was out of sight.

THE END OF THE SEARCH

'I really thought they'd found us when that man got up to the part we had blocked up,' said Jack.

'Yes – it was a jolly good thing we *did* block it up!' said Peggy. 'We would most certainly have been found if we hadn't!'

'And it was a good thing Mike sank the boat,' said Nora. 'If they had found a boat here they would have gone on looking for us till they'd found us.'

'I wonder what they meant when they said that such a surprise was waiting for us,' said Mike. 'It couldn't have been a nice surprise, I suppose?'

'Of course not!' said Peggy.

'They're almost out of sight,' said Nora. 'Do you think it's safe to get up and do a dance or something, Jack? I'm just longing to shout and sing and dance after being shut up in the cave for so long!'

'Yes, we're safe enough now,' said Jack. 'They won't come back. We can settle into the caves for the winter quite happily.'

'Shall we light a fire on the beach and have a good hot meal?' said Peggy. 'I think we could all do with one!'

'Right,' said Jack, and they set to work. Nora sang and danced about as she helped to fetch things. She felt so happy to think that they were safe, and that their secret island was their very own once more.

Soon they were eating as if they had never had a meal in their lives before. Then a loud moo from the hillside reminded them that Daisy was still there. So, leaving the girls to clear up, Jack sped off with Mike to get out Daisy and the hens.

'You're a good old cow, Daisy,' Jack said to her, rubbing her soft nose. 'We hoped you wouldn't moo when those men were hunting for us – but you knew better, and you mooed at them – and sent them off!'

The days were much shorter now, and night came early. It did not seem long before the sun went and the stars shone out in the sky. The children fetched the lantern from the cave and, taking their book, they went to Willow House. It was Nora's turn to read, and they all lay and listened to her. It was pleasant in Willow House with the lantern shining down softly, and the smell of the heather and bracken rising up. It was nice to be together and to know that the great hunt was over and they were safe.

'I'm sleepy,' said Jack, at last. 'Let's have some chocolate and a last talk and go to bed. You know, we shall soon have to think seriously of going to live in the caves. It won't be nice weather much longer!'

'We'll decide everything tomorrow,' said Mike sleepily, munching his chocolate.

They were soon asleep, for the day's excitement had

quite tired them out. But how lovely it was to wake the next day and know that the hunt was over and that they were safe for the winter. How they sang and joked and teased one another as they went down to bathe!

'Oooh!' said Nora, as she slipped into the water. 'It's getting jolly cold to bathe in the lake, Jack. Have we got to do this all the winter?'

'Of course not,' said Jack. 'We'll have to give it up soon – but it's nice whilst it's warm enough.'

That week the weather became really horrid. Storms swept over the lake and the children thought it looked just like the sea, with its big waves curling over and breaking on the beach with a crash. The waves ran right up the beach and it was impossible to make a fire there. The children got soaked with rain, and they had to dry their clothes as best they could by a fire they lighted outside the big cave. This was a good place for a fire, because the wind usually blew from the other direction and the fire was protected by the hill itself.

'I think we'll have to give up Willow House now and go to live in the caves,' said Jack one morning, after a very wild night. The wind had slashed at the trees all night long, the rain had poured down, and, to the children's dismay, a little rivulet of rain had actually come into Willow House from the back and had soaked the heather bed Peggy and Nora were lying on. The girls had had to get up in the middle of the night and go to the front room, where the boys slept. This was a squash, but the front room was dry.

The leaves were falling from the trees. Every tree and bush had flamed out into yellow, crimson, pink, brown or orange. The island was a lovely sight to see when the sun came out for an hour or two, for then its rays lighted up all the brilliant leaves, and they shone like jewels. But now the leaves were falling.

Leaves were dropping down in Willow House from the branches that made the roof. It was funny to lie in bed at night and feel a leaf drop lightly on to your cheek. Willow House looked different now that there were so few green or yellow leaves growing on the roof and walls. It was bare and brown.

Nora caught a cold and began to sneeze. Jack said they must move to the caves at once, or they would all get cold – and if they were ill, what would happen? There was no doctor to make them well!

They dosed Nora with hot milk and wrapped her up in the two new blankets Jack had bought in the village one week when he had been marketing. They set her at the back of the outer cave, with a candle beside her, for it was dim in that corner. She soon got better, and was able to help the others when they made their plans for living in the cave.

'We'll make this outer cave our living-room and bedroom!' Jack said, 'and the inner one shall be our storeroom. We'll always have a fire burning at the entrance, and that will warm us and cook our food. This is going to be rather fun! We shall be cave-people this winter!'

CHAPTER NINETEEN

Days in the Cave

THAT WEEK the children made all their plans for passing
the winter in the cave. Already all their stores were safely
placed in the inner cave. It was just a question of getting
the outer cave comfortable and home-like. Peggy was
wonderful at this sort of thing.

'You two boys must make a few shelves to put round
the cave,' she said. 'You can weave them out of stout twigs,
and put them up somehow. We will keep our books and
games there, and any odd things we want. You must
somehow manage to hang the lantern from the middle of
the roof. Then, in the corner over here we will have our
beds of heather and bracken. You boys can bring that
in, too. If it's wet we'll dry it by the fire. The bracken is
getting old and dry now – it should make a fine bed.'

Peggy swept up the floor of the cave with a brush made
of heather twigs, and then she and Nora threw fine sand
on it which they had brought from the beach. It looked
very nice. The boys brought in the heather and bracken
for the beds. Peggy arranged them comfortably, and then

threw a blanket over each bed but one. There were only three blankets – two new ones and one old one – so it looked as if someone must go without.

'What's the fourth bed going to have for a blanket?' asked Jack.

And then Peggy brought out a great surprise! It was a fur rug, made of rabbit skins that she had carefully cleaned, dried, and sewn together! How the others stared!

'But how lovely, Peggy!' said Jack. 'It's a most beautiful fur rug, and will be as warm as toast. We'll take it in turns to have it on at night.'

'Yes, that's what I thought,' said Peggy, pleased to find the others admired her rabbit rug so much. 'It was very hard to sew the skins together, but I did it at last. I thought it would be a nice surprise for when the cold weather came!'

Soon the cave began to look very homely indeed. The shelves were weighed down with the books and games. The lantern swung in the middle, and they all knocked their heads against it before they became used to it there! The beds lay neatly in the corners at the back, covered with blankets and the rabbit rug. In another corner stood the household things that Peggy was always using – the kettle, the saucepans, and so on.

And then Jack brought out a surprise – a nice little table

he had made by himself! He had found the old plank the children had brought with them months ago when they first came to the island, and had managed, by means of a saw he had bought during his marketing, to make a good little table for Peggy!

It was a bit wobbly. The four legs were made of tree branches, the straightest Jack could find, but it was difficult to get them just right. He had sawn the plank into pieces, and nailed them together to make a square top to the table, and this was very good. Peggy was delighted!

'Now we can have meals on the table!' she cried. 'Oh, that will be nice! And I can do my mending on the table, too – it will be much easier than crouching on the floor!'

'But what about chairs?' asked Nora. 'You can't sit up to the table without chairs!'

'I'm making stools,' said Jack – and so he was! He had found an old tree broken in two by the wind on the other side of the hill. With his saw he was sawing up the trunk, and each piece he sawed out was like a solid stool – just a piece of tree trunk, but nice and smooth to sit on!

The days passed very happily as they made the cave into a home. It was fun to sit on their little stools beside Jack's table and eat their meals properly there. It was fun to watch the fire burning at the entrance of the cave, getting brighter and brighter as night came on. It was lovely to lie on a soft heathery bed at the back of the cave, covered by a warm blanket or rabbit rug, and watch the fire gradually die down to a few glowing embers.

It was very cosy in the cave when the wind howled round the hillside. The light from the lantern shone down, and sometimes Peggy had an extra candle beside her when she sewed. The boys scraped at a bit of wood, carving something, or played a game with Nora. Sometimes they read out loud. The fire burnt brightly and lighted up the cave brilliantly every now and again when extra big flames shot up. It was great fun.

There was always plenty to do. Daisy still had to be milked each morning and evening. She seemed quite happy living in the grassy field, and the boys had built her a sort of shelter where she went at night. There were the hens to feed and look after. They were in a yard near the cave now. They were not laying so many eggs, but the children had plenty of stores and did not worry about eggs.

There was the usual cooking, washing, and clearing-up to do. There was water to be got from the spring. There was firewood to hunt for and pile up. Peggy liked to find pine cones because they burnt up beautifully and made such a nice smell.

November passed by. Sometimes there were lovely fine days when the children could sit out on the hillside and bask in the sun. Sometimes there were windswept days when the rain pelted down and the clouds raced across the sky, black and ragged. Then the lake was tossed into white-topped waves.

Mike and Jack had got the boat up again and mended it. They had pulled it up the beach as far as they could to be out of reach of the waves.

When December came, the children began to think of Christmas. It would be strange to have Christmas on the island!

'We'll have to decorate the cave with holly,' said Jack. 'There are two holly trees on the island, and one has red berries on. But there is no mistletoe.'

'Christmas will be funny with only just ourselves,' said Peggy. 'I don't know if I will like it. I like hearing carols sung, and seeing the shops all full of lovely things, and looking forward to Christmas stockings and crackers, and things like that.'

'Before our Daddy and Mummy flew off in their aeroplane and got lost, we used to have Christmas with them,' Nora said to Jack. 'It was lovely then. I remember it all!'

'I wish Daddy and Mummy hadn't gone away and got lost for ever,' said Mike. 'I did love them – they were so jolly and happy.'

DAYS IN THE CAVE

Jack listened as the three children told him all they had done at Christmas time when their father and mother had been with them. He had always lived with his old grandfather, who had never bothered about Christmas. To Jack this all seemed wonderful. How Mike, and Nora, and Peggy must miss all the happy and lovely things they used to do when they had their father and mother with them!

The boy listened and made up his mind about something. He would take the boat and row off to the end of the lake just before Christmas. He still had some money – and with that he would buy crackers, a doll for Nora, a new work-box for Peggy, something for Mike, and some oranges and sweets! They should have a fine Christmas!

He said nothing to the others about it. He knew that they would be terribly afraid that he might be caught again. But he did not mean to go to the same village as before. He meant to walk to the one five miles away, where he would not be known, and buy what he wanted there. He was sure he would be safe, for he meant to be very careful indeed!

December crept on. The days were dull and dreary. Jack planned to go off in the boat one morning. He would tell the others he was just going for a row to get himself warm. He would not tell them about his great surprise for them!

A good day came when the pale wintry sun shone down, and the sky was a watery blue. Peggy was busy clearing up after breakfast. Mike meant to rebuild Daisy's shelter, which had been rather blown about by the wind. Nora was going to look for pine cones.

'What are *you* going to do, Jack?' asked Peggy.

'Oh,' said Jack, 'I think I'll take the old boat out and go for a row to get myself warm. I haven't rowed for ages!'

'I'll come with you, Jack,' said Nora.

But Jack didn't want anyone with him! 'No, Nora,' he said, 'you go out and look for cones. I shall be gone a good while. Peggy, could you let me have some food to take with me?'

'Food!' said Peggy in amazement. 'However long are you going for, Jack?'

'Oh, just a few hours,' said Jack. 'Some exercise will do me good. I'll take my fishing line, too.'

'Well, put on your overcoat, then,' said Peggy. 'You'll be cold out on the windy lake.'

She put some rolls and a hard-boiled egg into a basket, together with a bottle of milk. Jack said goodbye and set off down the hillside. Nora came with him, half sulky at not being allowed to go in the boat.

'You might let me come, Jack,' she said.

'You can't come today, Nora,' said Jack. 'You will know why when I come back!'

He pushed off and rowed out on to the lake, which was not very rough that day. He rowed hard, and Nora soon left the beach and went to seek for cones. She thought she would try and see where Jack was fishing, after a time, and went to the top of the hill – but, try as she would, she could see no sign of the boat. She thought that very strange.

Hours went by, and Jack did not come back. The others waited for him, wondering why he had gone off alone and why he had not come back.

'Do you think he's gone to the village again to get anything?' asked Peggy at last. 'Nora says she couldn't see his boat anywhere on the lake when she looked – and if he was fishing anywhere near, we should easily see him!'

'Oh, dear!' said Mike, worried. 'If he goes to that village he'll be caught again!'

But Jack hadn't been caught. Something else had happened – something very extraordinary!

CHAPTER TWENTY

Jack Has a Great Surprise

WE MUST go back to Jack and find out what had been happening to him. He had been such a long time away from the island – far longer than he would have been if he had just gone shopping. What could have kept him?

Well, he had got safely in the boat to the far end of the lake, and had tied the boat up to a tree. Then he had slipped through the wood, and taken the road that led to the distant village, five miles away. It would take him nearly an hour and a half to get there, but what fun it would be to do a bit of shopping again!

The boy padded along the wintry road. It was muddy and cold, but he was as warm as toast. He jingled his money in his pocket and wondered if he could buy all he wanted to. He did badly want to get a doll for Nora, for he knew how much she would love it!

He carried the food Peggy had given him, and, when he got near the village, he sat up on a gate and ate it. Then off he went again. He did not think anyone would know him to be one of the runaways, for surely people had forgotten all about them by now! It was half a year since they had first run off to the island! But he was keeping a sharp look out in case he saw anyone looking at him too closely!

He went into the village. It was a big, straggling one, with a small High Street running down the middle. There were about six shops there. Jack went to look at them. He left the toy and sweet shop till last. He looked at the turkeys in the butcher's shop, some with red ribbons on. He looked into the draper's shop and admired the gay streamers that floated all about it to decorate it for Christmas. It was fun to see shops again.

And then he came to the toy shop. It was lovely! Dolls stood in the window with their arms stretched out as if they were asking people to buy them. A railway train ran on lines. A little Father Christmas stood in the middle, carrying a sack. Boxes of chocolate, tins of toffee, and big bottles of brightly coloured sweets were in the shop, too.

Jack stood gazing, wondering which doll to buy for Nora. He had already seen a nice little work-basket for Peggy, and had spied a book for Mike about boats. There was a box of red crackers at the back of the window, too, which he thought would do well for Nora. It would be such fun to pull them on Christmas Day in the cave, and wear paper hats there!

Jack went into the shop. It had two or three other people

there, for the shop was a post office, too, and people were sending off Christmas parcels. The shop assistant was weighing them – and it was a long business. Jack waited patiently, looking round at all the toys.

The people in the shop were talking to one another. At first Jack did not listen – and then he heard something that made him prick up his ears.

This is what he heard:

'Yes, it's a great pity those children were never found,' said one woman. Their father and mother are quite ill with grief, I've heard.'

'Poor things,' said the second woman. 'It's bad enough to come down in an aeroplane on a desert island, and not be found for two years – and then to come back safe to see your children – and learn that they've disappeared!'

Jack's eyes nearly dropped out of his head. What did this mean? Could it possibly – possibly – mean that Mike's father and mother had turned up again. Forgetting all about being careful, Jack caught hold of the arm of the first woman.

'Please,' he said, 'please tell me something. Were the three children you are talking about called Mike, Peggy and Nora – and is it *their* father and mother that have come back?'

The woman in the shop stared at the excited boy in

astonishment. 'Yes,' said the first woman. 'Those were the children's names. They disappeared in June with another boy, called Jack, and have never been found. And in August the missing father and mother were found far away on a Pacific Island, and brought back safely here. Their aeroplane had come down and smashed, and they had been living there until a ship picked them up.'

'But their children had gone,' said the shop assistant joining in, 'and it almost broke their hearts, for they had been worrying about them for months and longing to see them.'

'What do *you* know about all this?' suddenly said one of the women. 'You're not one of the children, are you?'

'Never mind about that,' said Jack impatiently. 'Just tell me one thing – where are the father and mother?'

'They are not far away,' said the shop assistant. 'They are staying at a hotel in the next town, hoping that the children will still be heard of.'

'What hotel?' said Jack eagerly.

'The Swan Hotel,' said the shop assistant, and then the women stared in amazement as Jack tore out of the shop at top speed, his eyes shining, and a look of the greatest excitement on his brown face!

He ran to the bus stop. He knew that buses went to the town, and he had only one thought in mind – to get to the

Swan Hotel and tell Mike's father and mother that their children were safe! Never in his life had Jack been so excited. To think that things would all come right like this, and he, Jack, was the one to tell the father and mother!

He jumped into the bus, and could not keep still. He leapt out of it when it rumbled into the town and ran off to the Swan Hotel. He rushed into the hall and caught hold of the hall-porter there.

'Where are Captain and Mrs Arnold?' he cried. Mike had often told him that his father was a captain, and he knew the children's surname was Arnold – so he knew quite well whom to ask for.

'Here, here, not so fast, young man,' said the porter, not quite liking the look of the boy in the old overcoat, and worn-out shoes. 'What do you want the Captain for?'

'Oh, tell me, please, where are they?' begged Jack – at that moment a man's voice said:

'Who's this asking for me? What do you want, boy?'

Jack swung round. He saw a tall, brown-faced man looking down at him, and he liked him at once, because he was so like Mike to look at.

'Captain Arnold! I know where Mike and Peggy and Nora are!' he cried.

The Captain stared as if he had not heard aright. Then he took Jack's arm and pulled him upstairs into a room where a lady sat, writing a letter. Jack could see she was the children's mother, for she had a look of Peggy and Nora about her. She looked kind and strong and wise, and Jack wished very much that she was his mother, too.

'This boy says he knows where the children are, Mary,' said the Captain.

What excitement there was then! Jack poured out his story and the two grown-ups listened without saying a word. When he had finished, the Captain shook hands with Jack, and his wife gave him a hug.

'You're a fine friend for our children to have!' said the Captain, his face shining with excitement. 'And you really mean to say that you have all been living together on that little island and nobody has found you?'

'Yes,' said Jack, 'and oh, sir, is it true that you and Mrs Arnold have been living on an island, too, till a ship picked you up?'

'Quite true,' said Captain Arnold, with a laugh. 'Our plane came down and smashed – and there we were, lost on an island in the Pacific Ocean! Little did we know that our children were going to live alone on an island, too! This sort of thing must be in the family!'

'John, we must go at once to them,' said Mrs Arnold, who was almost crying with joy. 'Quickly, this very minute. I can't wait!'

'We'd better get a proper boat,' said Jack. 'Our old boat is a leaky old thing now.'

It wasn't long before a car was brought round to the door, and Jack, Captain and Mrs Arnold were driving to the lakeside. They hired a big boat from a fisherman there, and set off to the secret island. Jack wondered and wondered what the children would say!

Meanwhile the three children were getting more and more worried! It was past teatime now, and getting dark. Where *could* Jack be?

'I can hear the splash of oars!' cried Peggy at last. They ran down to the beach, and saw the outline of the boat in the twilight coming near to the island. And then Mike saw that it was a bigger boat than their own – and there were three people in it, instead of one!

'That means Jack's been caught – and these people have been sent to get us!' he thought, and his heart sank. But then, to his amazement, he heard Jack's clear voice ringing out over the darkening water.

'Mike! Peggy! Nora! It's all right! I've brought a Christmas present for you!'

The three children stared. Whatever could Jack mean? But when the boat landed, and Captain and Mrs Arnold sprang out, they soon knew!

'Mummy! Oh, Mummy! And Daddy!' shrieked the

children, and flung themselves at their father and mother. You couldn't tell which were children and which were grown-ups, because they were all so mixed up. Only Jack was alone. He stood apart, looking at them – but not for long. Nora stretched out her hand and pulled him into the crowd of excited, happy people.

'You belong, too, Jack,' she said.

Everyone seemed to be laughing and crying at the same time. But at last it was so dark that no one could see anyone else. Jack lighted the lantern that Mike had brought down to the beach, and led the way to the cave. He badly wanted Captain and Mrs Arnold to see how lovely it was.

They all crowded inside. There was a bright fire crackling just outside, and the cave was warm and cosy. Jack hung the lantern up and placed two wooden stools for the children's parents. Peggy flew to heat some milk, and put out rolls of bread and some potted meat she had been saving up for Christmas. She did so want her mother to see how nicely she could do things, even though they all lived in a cave!

'What a lovely home!' said Mrs Arnold, as she looked round and saw the shelves, the stools, the table, the beds, and everything. The cave was very neat and tidy, and looked so cosy and friendly. How they all talked! How they jumped up and down and laughed and told first this thing and then the other! Only one thing made Captain and Mrs Arnold angry – and that was the tale of how unkind Aunt Harriet and Uncle Henry had been.

'They shall be punished,' said Captain Arnold, and that was all he said about them.

Daisy chose to moo loudly that night, and Captain Arnold laughed till the tears came into his eyes when he heard about the night that poor Daisy had had to swim behind the boat to the island! And when he heard how she had mooed and frightened away the people who had come to look for them, he laughed still more!

'Someone will have to write a book about your adventures,' he said. 'I never in my life heard anything like them. *We* didn't have such thrilling adventures on *our* island! We just lived with the native people there till a boat picked us up! Very dull indeed!'

Jack disappeared at that moment, and when he came back he carried a great load of heather. He flung it down in a corner.

'You'll stay with us tonight, won't you, Captain?' he said. 'We'd love to have you. Please do.'

'Of course!' said Captain Arnold. And Mrs Arnold nodded her dark head. 'We will all be together in the cave,' she said. 'Then we shall share a bit of your secret island, children, and know what it is like.'

JACK HAS A GREAT SURPRISE

So that night the children had visitors! They all fell asleep on their heather beds at last, happy, excited, and very tired. What fun to wake up tomorrow with their own father and mother beside them!

CHAPTER TWENTY-ONE

The End of the Adventure

MIKE AWOKE first in the morning. He sat up and remembered everything. There were his father and mother, fast asleep on their heathery bed in the corner of the cave! It was true then – he hadn't dreamt it all! They were alive and well, and had got their children again – everything was lovely.

Mike crept out to light the fire. He could not possibly go to sleep again. The day was just creeping in at the cave entrance. The sky was a very pale blue, and the sun was trying to break through a thin mist in the east. It was going to be fine!

When the fire was crackling merrily everyone woke up. Nora flung herself on her mother, for she could not believe she really had a mother again, and had to keep hugging her and touching her. Soon the cave was filled with talk and laughter.

Peggy and Nora got the breakfast. Mike showed his father the inner cave and their stores. Jack flew off to milk Daisy. The hens clucked outside, and Nora fetched in four brown eggs.

Fish from Jack's line, eggs, rolls, the rest of the potted meat, and a tin of peaches made a fine breakfast, washed down with hot tea. The fire died down and the sunshine came in at the cave entrance. Everyone went outside to see what sort of a day it was.

The lake sparkled blue below. The bare trees swung gently in the breeze. Nora told her mother all about the wild raspberries and strawberries and nuts, and Peggy chattered about the seeds they had planted, and the baskets they could make.

And then Captain Arnold said, 'Well, I think it's about time we were going.'

The children looked up at him. 'Going! What do you mean, Daddy? Leave our island?'

'My dears,' said Captain Arnold, 'you can't live here always – besides, there is no need for you to, now. You are not runaways any more. You are our own children that we love, and we must have you with us.'

'Yes,' said Mrs Arnold. 'We must all go back to a proper home, and you must go to school, my dears. You have been very brave and very clever – and very happy, too – and now you can have a lovely home with us, and we will all be happy together.'

'But what about Jack?' asked Nora, at once.

'Jack is ours, too,' said Mrs Arnold. 'I am sure his grandfather will be glad for us to have him for always. He shall have me for his mother, and your father shall be his, too! We will all be one big family!'

Jack wanted to say such a lot but he couldn't say a single word. It was very strange. His face just went red with joy, and he held Nora's hand so tightly that he hurt her without meaning to. He was just about the happiest boy in the world at that moment.

'Mummy, I shall so hate leaving our dear, dear island,' said Nora. 'And Willow House, too – and our cosy cave and the bubbling spring – and everything.'

'I think I might be able to buy the island for you,' said Daddy. 'Then, in the holidays you can always come here and run wild and live by yourselves if you want to. It shall be your very own.'

'Oh, Daddy!' shouted the children, in delight. 'We shan't mind going to school and being proper and living in a house if we've got the island to go back to in the holidays! Oh, what fun it will be!'

'But I think you must leave it now and come back home for Christmas,' said Mrs Arnold. 'We have our own old home to go back to – you remember it, don't you? Don't you think it would be nice to have Christmas there – and a Christmas pudding – and crackers – and stockings full of presents?'

'Yes, yes, yes!' shouted all the children.

'It's just what I longed for!' said Nora.

'I was going to buy you some red crackers yesterday, Nora,' said Jack, 'but I heard the great news before I had bought anything!'

'You shall all have red crackers!' said Captain Arnold, with a laugh. 'Now, what about getting off in the boat?'

'Just give us time to say goodbye to everything,' said Peggy. 'Mummy, come down and see Willow House. We made it ourselves and it's so pretty in the summer, because you see, it's a *live* house, and grows leaves all the time!'

In an hour's time everyone was ready to leave. The hens were bundled once more into a sack and were most annoyed about it. Daisy was left, and Captain Arnold said he would send a fisherman over for her. It was too cold for her to swim behind the boat. Most of the children's stores were left, too. They would be able to use them when they next went to the island.

Peggy took the rabbit rug she had made. That was too precious to leave. They brought the books too, because they had got fond of those. They had stored everything carefully in the inner cave, and thrown sacks over them in case of damp. They couldn't help feeling a bit sad to leave, although they knew they were going to their own happy home again.

At last everyone was in the boat. Captain Arnold pushed off and the sound of oars came to Daisy's ears as she stood pulling at the thin winter grass. She stood watching the boat as it bobbed away on the waves.

'Goodbye, dear secret island,' said Nora.

'Goodbye, goodbye!' said the others. 'We'll come back again! Goodbye, Daisy, goodbye, everything!'

'And now let's talk about all we're going to do at Christmas,' said Mrs Arnold, cheerfully, for she saw that the children were sad at leaving their beloved little island.

It was not long before the four children and their father and mother (for Jack counted them as his parents too, now) were settled happily in their own home. There was such a lot of excitement at first, for the children had to have new dresses, new suits, new underclothes, new socks, new shoes! Mrs Arnold said that although Peggy had really done her best to keep them tidy, they were quite dropping to pieces!

So off they went shopping, and came back feeling as grand as kings and queens, all dressed up in their new things! Peggy looked fine in a blue coat and skirt with a little blue hat. Nora wore red, and the two boys had suits and overcoats of dark blue.

THE END OF THE ADVENTURE

Jack felt strange in his. It was the first time in his life he had ever had anything new of his own to wear, for he had always gone about in somebody's old things before! He felt very grand indeed.

The children looked at one another and burst out laughing.

'How different we look now!' said Mike. 'Think of our dirty old rags on the island! But it's good to be really properly dressed again – and the girls *do* look nice!'

It was strange at first to sleep in a proper bed again. The girls slept in a pretty room and had a little white bed each. The boys slept in the next room, and had two brown beds. At first they all wondered where they were when they awoke in the morning, but after a few days they got used to it.

Christmas drew near. They all went out to buy presents for one another. It was most exciting. They went to London and marvelled at the great shops there. They watched all kinds of ships and boats sailing along in a big tank. They saw model trains tearing round and round a little countryside, going through tunnels, stopping at stations, just like a real train. It was all very exciting after living such a peaceful life on the island.

Christmas was lovely. They hung up their stockings at the end of their beds – and in the morning what fun they had finding the things packed tightly in the long stockings! In the girls' – oranges, sweets, nuts, soaps and bath bubbles – and in the boys' were all kind of things, too. Bigger presents were at the foot of the bed, and *how* excited all the children were unpacking them!

'This is better than Christmas in the cave!' said Nora, unpacking a great big smiling doll with curly golden hair. 'Oh, Jack! Did you really buy this for me? Oh, how lovely, lovely, lovely!'

Soon the bedrooms were full of dolls, books, trains, balls, aeroplanes and motor cars! It was the loveliest Christmas morning the children had ever had – and certainly Jack had never in his life known one like it! He just simply couldn't believe his luck.

'You deserve it all, Jack,' said Nora. 'You were a good friend to us when we were unhappy – and now you can share with us when we are happy.'

There was a Christmas tree after tea, with more presents – and as for the crackers, you should have seen them! Red ones and yellow ones, blue ones and green ones! Soon everyone was wearing a paper hat, and how the children laughed when Captain Arnold pulled a cracker and got a tiny aeroplane out of it!

'Well, you can't fly away in *that* Daddy,' cried Peggy.

'You won't ever fly away again, Daddy, will you?' said

THE END OF THE ADVENTURE

Nora, suddenly frightened in case her father and mother should fly off again and be lost, so that the four children would be alone once more.

'No, never again,' said her father. 'Mummy and I have made such a lot of money out of our flying now, that we can afford to stay at home and look after you. We shall never leave you again!'

It was four happy children who went to bed that night. The boys left the door open between their room and the girls', so that they might all talk to one another till they fell asleep. They could not get out of this habit, for they had always been able to talk to one another in bed on the island.

'It's been a lovely day,' said Peggy sleepily. 'But I do just wish something now.'

'What?' asked Mike.

'I do just wish we could all be back in our cosy cave on our secret island for five minutes,' said Peggy.

'So do I,' said everyone, and they lay silent, thinking of the happy days and nights on the island.

'I shall never, never forget our island,' said Nora. 'It's the loveliest place in the world, I think. I hope it isn't feeling lonely without us! Goodnight, secret island! Wait for us till we come again!'

'Goodnight, secret island!' said the others. And then they slept, and dreamt of their island – of the summer days when they would go there once more, and live merrily and happily alone, in the hot sunshine – of winter days in the cosy cave – of cooking over a campfire – and sleeping soundly on heathery beds. Dear secret island, only wait, and you shall have the children with you once again!

BONUS BLYTON!

Turn the page for exciting extras
by Enid Blyton to read and share!

The Secret Island was first serialised in the weekly magazine *Enid Blyton's Sunny Stories*, between September 1937 and February 1938. Here's the letter Enid wrote to her readers, introducing *The Secret Island*, and the first page of the adventure. Both pages are just as they appeared in the magazine in 1937!

OLD THATCH,

DEAR CHILDREN,—

　　To-day the new story begins, and I do hope you will like it. It is a most exciting tale about four children who run away to a secret island they know, and the story will tell how they live there alone, and all the adventures they have. I hope you will not be too sad that "The Wishing-Chair" is finished. You will soon be able to get all the Wishing-Chair Stories in a book. I will tell you all about it when it is ready.

　　I have sent a prize to Angela Diss, whose nice little poem is over the page. I hope she likes the picture that has been drawn for her poem. I do. Other prizes have been sent to the lucky winners of Competition No. 31. You will find their names on page 31. The new competition is a good one. Try your luck at it, and see if you can win a prize.

　　Wouldn't you like a magic pencil like the one in the poem on page 3 of the cover? I am sure you would! So would I!

　　Much love to you all from

Enid Blyton

(No. 37.)

1.
The BEGINNING of the ADVENTURES

MIKE, Peggy, and Nora were sitting in the fields, talking together. They were very unhappy. Nora was crying, and would not stop.

As they sat there, they heard a low call. "Coo–ee!"

"There's Jack," said Mike. "Dry your eyes, Nora. Jack will cheer you up!"

A boy came running by the hedge and sat down by them. He had a face as brown as a berry and bright blue eyes that shone with mischief.

"Hallo!" he said. "What's up, Nora? Crying again?"

My Very First Garden

This is an extract from The Story of My Life, *Enid Blyton's autobiography, published in 1952. Like the children in The Secret Island, Enid Blyton loved growing things outside. In this chapter, she tells her readers about her first garden and what she planted in it.*

One of the things you sometimes ask me is whether I ever had a little garden as a child. You usually ask me that question when you yourself have just been given a garden and you want to know what seeds to plant, and so on.

It is really lovely to have a little garden for yourself when you are small. But I do so hope that if you are given one, it will not be in a horrid shady little patch where nothing will grow – but will be a nice, sunny piece with good soil. It is so very disappointing when you are a child, and have your first garden, to find that nothing can grow well in it.

I had a very small one, but it was sunny and the soil

was good. My father loved his garden, and he thought we children should have patches too. I can remember my little patch perfectly.

It was square, and ran from the path to the wall. I knew what to do because I had often watched my father in the big garden, and had helped him.

I dug it over well, as deeply as I could. I then got a trowel and broke up the earth as finely as possible, and made it smooth and level. It looked very nice, I thought.

And then came the exciting part. What should I plant in it? It was April, and everyone was planting seeds. I must plant seeds too. But I only had a penny a week and that wouldn't buy many seeds.

So my father made a bargain with me. 'If you want anything badly, you have to work for it,' he said. 'I will give you enough money to buy your own seeds, if you earn it. I want my bicycle cleaned – cleaned well, too. And I want the weeds cleared from that bed over there. If the work is done properly, it is worth sixpence to me, and that will buy you six penny packets of seeds.'

How I worked! I kept thinking of candy-tuft and Shirley poppies and mignonette as I rubbed up that bicycle, and I thought of clarkia and nasturtiums and virginia stock as I pulled up handfuls of weeds.

So I earned the money for my first garden, and how

proud I was when I went to spend my sixpence on those gay packets of seeds. I got the six I wanted. They were only a penny a packet in those days.

My very first garden – how I loved it. Nobody knew how much I loved it. Well, you might know, perhaps, because some of you feel exactly the same about such things as I felt. You don't tell anyone at all, you just think about them and hug them to yourself.

I planted my seeds. I read the instructions well and followed them exactly. I made labels. I planned my little patch carefully – the tiny virginia stock at the front edge. The candytuft and mignonette next. Then the clarkia and the Shirley poppies. And at the back, the nasturtiums, which were climbing ones. I planned to let them climb up the wall on string.

I looked each day to see if the seeds were coming up. Then one warm morning after a rainy night, lo and behold, there were little green lines and patches in my garden – the seeds were coming up!

I told everybody. I told my family, and I told my teacher at school. I told the milkman and I told anyone who would listen. So you can guess how excited I was. But it is exciting when the very first seeds you have ever planted actually come up. I still find it exciting when I see my seeds poking up now.

My first garden was a great success. It was a good summer, and all my plants flourished well. My father showed me how to thin out my seedlings. 'Better to have a few fine plants, than lots of weaklings,' he said.

So I had a border of virginia stock that somehow reminded me of those little seed like sweets called hundreds and thousands. I had patches of candytuft, spires of graceful, brilliant clarkia, dancing poppies of all colours, sweet-smelling mignonette, and many hardy nasturtiums that climbed high over the wall, thick with orange flowers. That was my first garden.

The next year I tried a few plants, as well as seeds. An aunt came to see us and gave me the magnificent sum of one shilling. That was riches to me – almost like five shillings would be to you nowadays.

I was most extravagant with my shilling, and actually didn't put even a penny into my money-box pig, though I quite meant to. I bought two button-daisy plants, one pink, one white. Do you know those little button daisies? Most children love them. I bought a pansy plant too, because I always thought that pansies had faces that looked at me.

Some of you may know what I mean. Pansies do seem to look up at you. Some flowers never look at you – snowdrops for instance. My pansy had a deep purple face with yellow in the centre, and wavy edges. I can still see it quite clearly, and although I have grown hundreds of pansy faces since, I still think that one was the loveliest.

I also bought a tiny lavender plant that cost me threepence – and in two years' time it was a magnificent bush, and I was able to pick enough lavender from it to fill a little bag for my mother's handkerchiefs.

The next year I had bigger ideas, and tried things like radishes and lettuces, and grew one solitary runner bean up the wall with my nasturtiums. It did very well too. I picked at least twenty pods from it! We had them one dinnertime, and I was very pleased when my mother said they were the nicest beans we'd ever had.

My lettuces were magnificent too – they were the tall kind, called Cos lettuce, and I tied them up just like my father tied his, so that they would get nice hearts. I shall never in my life forget having the first one at teatime with brown bread-and-butter and salt. I don't tell this sort of thing to grown-ups, of course, but you children will understand exactly how I felt. My radishes were also delicious – 'nice and crumpy', as one of my brothers said; hot too, and juicy.

I am always telling children to try and grow things if they can – seeds, plants, salads, vegetables, it doesn't matter what. It's like magic to see the seeds turning into little green plants, to see four tiny lettuce leaves grow into a fat, juicy lettuce, and tiny sprig of lavender become a great bush. People are happy when they grow things, especially children. If ever I was unhappy as a child I used to go and garden, and I still do the same if I am worried about anything.

Some people have what is called the 'green thumb'. That is, anything will grow for them, even if they just 'dib' it in. Other people are not so lucky – they haven't a 'green thumb', so nothing grows well.

But I have noticed that anyone who really loves flowers or gardens or messing about with the earth has a green thumb. Those who love flowers know how to handle them, gently, lovingly, roots, leaves, bulbs and all. And plants grow well for them, and always will. I do hope you have a green thumb when you garden. It does make such a difference!

Do have a garden if you can – but once you begin one, keep on with it. So often I hear a grown-up say: 'Well, John did have a nice little garden – but he soon got tired of it, you know, so it's part of the big garden now.'

What I learnt in my garden when I was small has made it possible for me to run my own big garden now. There is not a thing I don't know about my garden. When, for two years, we had no gardener at all, we carried on ourselves

– we mowed the lawns, and weeded the paths, we planted the seeds, we pruned the roses. We had most magnificent vegetables, and the best crop of fruit we had ever had.

But I know I could never have done it if my father hadn't given me that small patch long ago. I made my own 'green thumb' by working in it, learning about all the plants, and trying everything I could. What fun I had – just as much fun as you will have too, I hope.

Don't miss the next thrilling Secret Stories adventure!

THE SECRET STORIES

The Secret of Spiggy Holes

When Peggy, Mike, Nora and Jack find a secret to unravel, their adventures soon begin.

The Arnold children are on holiday at the seaside. While exploring the Spiggy Holes caves, they discover a secret passage to the Old House on the cliff. But is the Old House hiding secrets of its own?